Praise for the No. 2 Feline Detective Agency series

'**Original and intriguing...** a world without people which cat lovers will enter and enjoy' P. D. James

'**Deliciously clever and a true delight**' Laura Thompson

'**I loved it.** The whole concept is just so "real"!' Barbara Erskine

'Mandy Morton's Feline Detective Agency instigates a new genre, both **wonderful and surreal**' Maddy Prior

'There's **so much heart** in this book as well as a **cracking good plot**. Can't wait for the next one!' Barbara Nadel

'The world that Morton has created is **irresistible**' Publishers Weekly

'Witty and smart. **Prepare to be besotted**' M. K. Graff

'Mandy Morton's series is both **charming and whimsical**' Barry Forshaw

'Hettie Bagshot might be a new face at the scene of a crime, but already **she could teach most fictional detectives a thing or two**' The Hunts Post

What readers are saying about the series:

'This series is **the perfect warm, fluffy cosy mystery read** for fans of Agatha Crispy-style mysteries and cat-lovers alike'

'**True escapism into a world of pies, cakes and cats** while somehow smuggling a truer reflection of the real world than much human detective fiction'

'A deceptively nasty murder wrapped up in a cardigan, and served by the fire with tea and cake. **A delight from beginning to end**'

'Hilarious and captivating'

'**The cat world's answer to the cosy crime novel**, with bags of charm and characters you don't want to leave behind'

'**I love this series** and am waiting with a warmed pastry, a hot mug of something, and a crackling fire for the next in the series'

The No. 2 **FELINE** Detective Agency

SIX TAILS AT MIDNIGHT

MANDY MORTON

This edition published in 2025 by Farrago,
an imprint of Duckworth Books Ltd

1 Golden Court,
Richmond TW9 1EU,
United Kingdom

www.farragobooks.com

A catalogue record for this book is available from the
British Library.

Printed and bound in Great Britain by CPI Ltd, Croydon, CR0 4YY

The authorised representative in the EEA is Easy Access System
Europe, Mustamäe tee 50, 10621 Tallinn, Estonia.

Print ISBN: 9781788425490
e-ISBN: 9781788425506

For Nicola, Betsey and Stanley and in memory of Scampi, a fine hotelier

Chapter One
Away for Christmas

Hettie Bagshot had never been keen on the prospect of going away for Christmas. Since settling in to Betty and Beryl Butter's storeroom at the back of their popular bakery, she had finally found a place she could call home. Along with her best friend, Tilly Jenkins, she had created The No. 2 Feline Detective Agency, and – after a bit of a shaky start – the business was blooming. Before meeting up with Hettie one Christmas Eve, Tilly had suffered the indignities and dangers of being a homeless cat; now she was the home*maker* and had turned the Butter sisters' storeroom into a cosy bedsitter with all the comforts a cat could desire, with the added bonus of a daily pie and as much coal as their small fire could consume in return for the very low rent they paid to their landladies.

Betty and Beryl Butter were two white cats from Lancashire who had come south to the town to seek their fortune. To say they were born with flour on their paws would be an understatement: their mother had schooled her daughters in the making of pies, pastries, cakes and breads as soon as they could wield a rolling pin. Buying up the town's old run-down bakery with the money their mother left them had started as an adventure; now, they had become legends in their own mixing bowls and the townsfolk flocked to their shop on a daily basis, buying up their freshly baked goods by three in the afternoon.

The lead-up to Christmas had been busy for the Butters, and for Hettie and Tilly. Betty and Beryl had been flat out since Halloween, creating seasonal treats and duplicating them in huge numbers for their customers. Hettie and Tilly had been engrossed in a nasty case of poison pen letters being circulated around the town and had caught the perpetrator fair and square with the help of Squeak, the town's postcat. The culprit had been apprehended as she posted one of her venomous notes in the letter box opposite the bakery. Triumphant from solving yet another case, Hettie had decided that their detective agency would take a long and well-earned break over the Christmas holidays, giving her and Tilly time to eat, drink, be merry and doze by a winter fire.

Traditionally, Hettie, Tilly and their friend Bruiser – who drove their red motorbike and sidecar and had once slept rough but now lived in a shed at the bottom of the Butters' garden – would celebrate Christmas Day with Betty and Beryl in their flat above the bakery, where their table groaned with every festive delight imaginable. But back at the beginning of December Betty had made a shock announcement. 'Sister and I have been thinking. As we'll be baking ourselves stupid up until Christmas, we thought we'd treat ourselves to Christmas away from the town and, 'cause we think of you as family, we'd like to take you all with us.'

Tilly and Bruiser had been delighted at the prospect, but Hettie felt immediately unsettled and, as Christmas approached and the Butters' plans were rolled out, her anxiety increased. The Butters had called a series of meetings to discuss the various possibilities of where they might go and it was eventually decided that The Fishgutter's Arms beyond the Much-Purrings would be a suitable venue. The vote was easily carried, although Hettie chose to abstain on the basis of a lack of detail over the contents of the Christmas dinner and the fact that Beryl had found the place in a small, understated advertisement in the *Daily Snout*.

The final meeting was to be held on the day before Christmas Eve, to 'dot the mince pies and cross the milky teas' as Betty had put it.

Chapter Two
Operation Getaway

'I think the tree is really lovely this year,' said Tilly, wobbling on a chair as she reached up to place the star on the top, 'and those new baubles we bought in Meridian Hambone's January sale are so sparkly.'

Hettie looked up from her armchair, where she'd been dozing by the fire. 'I don't know why you're bothering as we won't be here to see it, but I agree you've made a good job of it. It's much nicer than Lavender Stamp's tree at the post office. Hardly a bauble to be seen and she's put those awful gingerbread biscuits on it again, with half of them missing their heads, and those terrible tartan bows. I mean, what's that got to do with Christmas? The Christmas spirit is dead and buried in her post office, unless you count the bottles of cream sherry she consumes between issuing postal orders and insulting her customers.'

There was no love lost between Hettie and the town's postmistress, and Lavender Stamp's reputation for being a cantankerous, bad-tempered curmudgeon went before her. Her attitude towards her customers could only be described as spiteful, but as she was the only postal outlet in the town she had become a necessary evil.

'I think the tartan is for Hogmanay,' suggested Tilly, 'but I know what you mean about the sherry. There was a terrible sound of breaking glass when her bin was being emptied the other day. It must have been all her empties but I do feel a bit sorry for her. I expect she'll be on her own this year.'

'Well, at least she won't be crashing in on the Butters' Christmas dinner like she usually does. It's the only good thing about us all going away.'

There was a polite knock on the door and Tilly opened it to Bruiser. 'I thought I'd better come an' collect you fer the meetin' upstairs,' he said, giving the tree a look of admiration. 'The Butters 'ave closed up fer the day so we're all officially on 'oliday.'

Tilly clapped her paws with delight as Hettie reluctantly clambered down from her armchair. 'Quite frankly, I'll be glad when it's over this year,' she said. 'All the fuss and nonsense over packing to go away – meetings, road maps and, according to the weather cat on the TV, a heavy fall of snow is expected for tomorrow. I just hope The Fishgutter's Arms can offer roaring fires and decent food.'

'I'm sure it will be lovely,' said Tilly, picking up her notepad and pencil in case she needed to jot anything down, 'and I thought we could have an "at-home Christmas" when we get back. I'm leaving all the presents under the tree here so we don't have to pack them to take with us.'

Hettie brightened at the prospect of an 'at-home Christmas' and followed Tilly and Bruiser upstairs to the Butter sisters' flat for the final meeting of 'Operation Getaway', as it was now known.

In spite of being so busy at the bakery all day, Betty and Beryl had prepared a high tea for their fellow travellers and the meeting got off to a flying start with Tilly appreciatively reeling off the contents of the Butters' hostess trolley. 'I'll start with the sandwiches,' she said, sniffing at the fillings. 'We've got salmon paste, luncheon meat and sardine, all with the crusts cut off, mince pies, sausage rolls, coconut haystacks with a cherry on the top, buttered malt loaf and a huge bowl of crisps!'

'Sorry there's not much,' said Betty, bustling in from the kitchen with a teapot, followed by her sister with a tray of cups. 'We've been so busy in the bakery these past few days we've hardly had time to eat ourselves, have we, sister?'

Beryl nodded in agreement. 'And we've had to do all those extra sausage rolls and mince pies for Malkin and Sprinkle's "tastes extra nice" range, as well as their regular order of savouries,' she said, putting the cups down on the table. 'It was a blessing you recommending us to the local department store food hall all those years ago, but they seem to have gone into overdrive this Christmas and we've hardly been able to keep up.'

Hettie took the compliment at the same time as loading her plate with sandwiches. For her, suggesting the Butters' pies to Mr Malkin and Mr Sprinkle had been lucky, as Betty and Beryl had returned the favour by offering their storeroom to her for a very low rent and welcoming Tilly and Bruiser into their hospitable orbit. Their generosity had extended to building a shed for Bruiser and Miss Scarlet, the much-loved mode of transport for Hettie and Tilly's investigations.

'I think I'll start with a coconut haystack,' said Tilly, who could never be described as conventional. It quite simply never occurred to her that savouries should usually come before sweet; her years of being homeless, out in the cold, scavenging other cats' leftovers, had taught her that food was food; now that life was easier, she was in the happy position of pleasing herself. She nibbled round the cake until only the cherry was left, then triumphantly poked it into her mouth with sublime satisfaction before reaching for another one.

Tea was soon over, and the five cats diligently cleaned their whiskers and paws of any residues before Betty took control of the meeting, offering an itinerary designed to make their departure the following day a simple, straightforward affair. 'Now then,' she said, taking up a commanding position next to an imposing silver Christmas tree, tastefully decorated in red and gold baubles with not a tartan bow in sight, 'sister and I will take the Morris and you three can follow on in Miss Scarlet.'

'Wouldn't it be easier if we all squashed into the Morris?' Hettie interrupted. 'The weather looks pretty bad for tomorrow.'

The two sisters shared a look before Beryl chimed in, 'We're packing everything but the kitchen sink, so the back seat will be full up. We don't want to leave anything to chance.'

'Well, I'm very happy to travel in Miss Scarlet,' said Tilly, who loved the motorbike and sidecar and had named it after her favourite board game character. Hettie and Tilly had never quite mastered the motorbike – not that they'd ever tried that hard – but the luxury of the sidecar was a different experience altogether and as Bruiser was a real biker cat he was in his element driving them around. 'Will you have room to take my tartan shopper in the Morris?'

'Of course we will,' said Betty, 'and you'll need a few changes of clothes, as we'll have Christmas Eve dinner, Christmas Day lunch and Boxing Day. We may as well make an effort and get ourselves done up.'

Hettie groaned at the thought; clothes had never been her first consideration. During her music days, she'd had to wear so many changes of stage clothes on tour that now she liked nothing better than to hang out in the comfort of her dressing gown on days off. She had already resolved to let Tilly choose something for her from the bottom drawer of their filing cabinet, where they kept all their clothes.

'I'm takin' me two best waistcoats an' that Christmas bow tie Tilly bought me last year,' said Bruiser, keen to show he was making an effort. Tilly announced that she would be packing her three best cardigans, all with hoods, in case The Fishgutter's Arms turned out to be a bit bleak.

Satisfied that the clothes issue had been dealt with, Betty pushed on with the route they would take. 'It should be lovely travelling through the Much-Purring villages at this time of year, as they always make such a grand effort at Christmas.'

Bruiser nodded and pulled a map from his pocket, opening it out across the now empty hostess trolley. His paw traced the route he'd planned. 'We'll 'ave ta go through Much-Purrin'-on-the-Rug an' Much-Purrin'-on-the-Blanket before we join the B165 'ere at Scratchers Cross, then it's on past Dead Bones Dyke till we get to Gallows Edge Drove. I went there once in me wanderin's. It's where they used to 'ang cats in the old days. I reckon it was quite a spectacle with folks comin' from all over ta watch. They used ta save up the murderers for mass executions so cats could 'ave a proper day out with a fair an' everythin'.'

'Charming,' said Hettie. 'Nothing like a day out at the gallows. Just think – you could watch your neighbour swing and win a goldfish at the same time.'

The assembled company was more than used to Hettie's sarcasm and Bruiser continued with his route plan, tapping his claw on the circle he'd marked in red which he was confident showed where The Fishgutter's Arms was located. 'It's pretty strange out that way,' he said. 'Fenland country's full of odd folk. Then there's that big old cathedral stuck out there. They call it the ship of the fens. That whole area was nothin' but water once till some cat came along and drained it all. It's burstin' with myths and legends – and celery, of course.'

'Celery!' spluttered Hettie, draining her teacup.

'Yup, on account of the black soil,' said Bruiser. 'Carrots grow well out there too.'

'No wonder the fen cats are odd if all they have to rely on is celery and carrots,' Hettie pointed out. 'I've never been able to trust a cat who enjoys vegetables.'

'But the myths and legends sound interesting,' said Tilly, picking the coconut out of her teeth with one of her claws. 'I hope The Fishgutter's is haunted, especially at Christmas.'

'You've been to one too many of Irene Peggledrip's séances,' said Hettie. 'I think you should leave the supernatural to Mr Dickens at this time of year.'

The conversation had veered off in an unexpected direction and Betty was keen to bring the focus back to their Christmas holiday. 'As Hettie has mentioned, the forecast is for snow later tomorrow, so I think we'd better leave around ten and give ourselves plenty of time to get to The Fishgutter's before travelling conditions become difficult.'

Beryl nodded, keen to illustrate the point. 'Do you remember that Christmas when we got snowed in and had to spend Christmas Day at that church at the bottom of Pendle Hill, sister? We'd all gone to midnight mass – sung our hearts out, we did – and just as we were leaving to return home a giant snowball rolled down Pendle Hill and virtually swallowed up the church. Mother was beside herself, as she'd left a joint of beef cooking in her Aga.

The vicar, who suffered from claustrophobia, was distraught and we had to calm him down by forcing him to drink a whole bottle of altar wine. Then he was sick over the brand-new kneelers that Mrs Tap and her ladies had embroidered that autumn.'

'So how did you get out?' asked Tilly, keen to hear the end of the story.

It was Betty who finished the tale as Beryl wheeled the trolley into the kitchen to set about the washing up. 'Well, we sat for most of the night in our pews thankful for our good wool coats, and as the sun came up on that Christmas morning the stained glass threw the most magical shafts of coloured light across us. Paisley Stanhope struck up a medley of Christmas tunes on his organ and we all joined in, except for the Reverend Crouch who had passed out and was sleeping it off in the vestry. We kept our spirits up by playing guessing games and charades until teatime, when we heard the sound of Flavia Ashton's tractor. Flavia ran a farm across the top of Pendle. Bit of a recluse, really, but a good sort if you were in trouble. Anyway, she spent the best part of Christmas night digging us out of the church and we were all home safe and sound by midnight – except for the kneelers, of course.'

'What about the beef?' asked Hettie, getting her priorities right.

'Let's just say that when Mother opened the Aga and waved the smoke away, she offered us one of her pearls of wisdom. When it's brown it's done and when it's black it's buggered!'

Chapter Three
Christmas Eve

Tilly woke early. It was barely light and there were just enough embers in the fire to coax it into life by adding sticks and some small lumps of coal. She switched on the Christmas tree lights, which instantly brightened the room, lifting her spirits and adding to the excitement of the day ahead. She scraped the ice from the window that overlooked the Butters' backyard, marvelling at its patterns; Jack Frost had been busy with his claws overnight. The yard was white with the winter frost, echoing the scenes depicted in the many Christmas cards they'd received. A robin pecked at the window, hopping from one foot to another on the sill before flying off to a holly bush to breakfast on its berries. Hettie slept on as Tilly fetched her tartan shopper from its home in the hallway beside the bread ovens. The ovens were strangely silent and Tilly felt a little uneasy; since coming to live with Hettie, the sound of the bread ovens – fired up at four-thirty every morning – had been comforting, reminding her of being safe and warm as she turned over in her fleecy blankets and went back to sleep. Even on Sundays, the Butter sisters would bake in order to get ahead of the new week's orders, but today was different.

Christmas Eve was a special day for Hettie and Tilly. It was the day they'd met several years ago, Tilly curled up in a shop doorway, starving and covered in newspapers to keep out the bitter cold, and Hettie bored and out for a stroll on the snowy streets. Their friendship had been forged over a pork pie that Hettie had taken from her pocket and shared with Tilly before taking her home to her bedsit behind the bakery. The special bond the two tabbies had formed had become unbreakable, and although they were very different in character, they complemented each other in every way. Hettie was prone to dark moods, unsociable and often frustrated with the world around her. Tilly was mild-mannered, keen to make the best of everything and could find joy in each new day no matter what it dealt her. She was exactly what Hettie needed and understood her like no other cat ever had. Hettie had been Tilly's salvation: she had quite simply saved her life and given her a home and a friendship built on loyalty, trust and love, although Hettie would never admit to it.

Tilly had laid out the clothes on the table the night before, making sure that Hettie had some suitable best outfits for the holiday. She'd selected the monogrammed pyjamas that the Butters had bought them last Christmas and had also assembled some favourite festive snacks that she'd purchased from Malkin and Sprinkle earlier in the week. She had a fondness for sugared almonds, not shared by her teeth, and Hettie loved nut brittle; there was a box of Turkish delight to share with Bruiser and a vintage celebration tin of Playbox Biscuits for midnight feasts in their room. As the weather cat had promised snow, she'd gathered together a collection of mittens, hats and scarves in case they needed to walk off their Christmas lunch. She added Hettie's catnip pipe and pouch to the collection, with one of Agatha Crispy's shockers for herself to read, and packed it all into her tartan shopper.

Now that the small fire was behaving in a more positive frame of mind, Tilly crossed to the kettle to make the tea in hopes that a cheery blaze might inspire Hettie to wake up. Just as the kettle was coming to the boil, reinforcements arrived in the shape of Betty Butter, wearing her best housecoat and slippers, carrying a tray of bacon baps. 'There you go – a nice bit of back bacon with extra sauce, and sister has slipped an egg in as it's Christmas Eve so mind how you eat them as things could get messy. I've delivered one to Bruiser – he's already up and dressed and polishing Miss Scarlet. We'll see you outside the bakery at ten and we'll follow on in the Morris as Bruiser knows the way.'

Betty left Tilly to the unenviable task of waking Hettie, who was beginning to stir due to the sudden smell of bacon permeating their room. Tilly made two mugs of milky tea and carried one of them with a breakfast bap over to Hettie's chair. 'Breakfast!' she said, as gently as she could. 'A bacon bap and a milky tea.'

Hettie lifted her head out of the tangle of blankets and blinked. She'd been having a rather odd dream where she'd been tasked with picking a whole field of celery while Bruiser, wearing one of his best waistcoats, stood by with a stopwatch. She sat up, rubbed her eyes with her paws and focused on the bacon bap that Tilly had rested on the arm of her chair. She glanced over at the clock on the sideboard and was horrified to see that it was only eight o'clock – a good two hours before her normal wake-up time.

Tilly collected her own tea and her breakfast and settled herself on her blanket, waiting for the usual bad-tempered rhetoric with which Hettie started most of her days. She wasn't disappointed and today the subject matter included fine dining. 'The thing is,' Hettie began, 'Christmas is a time for being by your own fireside, with the cats who are close to you and lots of treats and presents. It's not about wearing posh clothes and putting on airs and graces at the dinner table. Anyway, in my experience posh clothes rarely fit, especially after a big dinner. They're too tight and uncomfortable, guaranteeing a severe bout of indigestion.'

Tilly giggled at her friend but let her continue, as she was keen to explore her own bacon bap. The egg had already begun to escape and was rapidly covering her paws, which added to the intensity of her enjoyment.

'It seems to me,' Hettie continued, 'that we know nothing about this Fishgutter's place. I mean, it's stuck out in the middle of nowhere, surrounded by fields of celery and carrots, in a place where no cat should stray if they were in their right mind. Not exactly the go-to place to spend Christmas. I honestly don't know what the Butters were thinking of. They like their comforts as much as we do.'

There was a crisis building on Tilly's blanket, and she was no longer listening to Hettie as her immediate attention was drawn to the escaped egg yolk that had forced its way out of the bap onto her paws and was now sliding down her chest onto her bedding. The more she tried to contain the disaster, the worse it got. Realising that help was needed, Hettie threw off her blankets and padded to the sink, where she wetted a tea towel and offered it to Tilly, returning to her chair to concentrate on her own bacon bap. In company, Tilly was persuaded not to choose food that behaved badly in her overlarge paws, but in the privacy of her own home she allowed herself the luxury of consuming and being consumed by her meals with sheer joy. She'd spent far too many years going without and had a lot to make up for.

Hettie made short work of her breakfast, daring her egg not to stray anywhere but into her mouth. Tilly finished cleaning herself up in the sink before selecting one of her older cardigans for travelling, having packed her three best ones in the tartan shopper. The two cats tidied their room and Hettie pulled on the clothes she'd worn the day before; by a quarter to ten, they were both ready to head out into the high street. Tilly took one last wistful look at the Christmas tree before turning its lights off, telling it that they would return very soon for their 'at-home Christmas'. The two friends put on their coats and scarves and left their own small Christmas behind to venture into the unknown.

The high street was bustling with last minute shoppers and they could hear strains of a brass band playing carols further down the road in front of Malkin and Sprinkle. Several cats were picking through Christmas trees outside Meridian Hambone's hardware store, hoping for a Christmas Eve bargain, and a couple of disgruntled customers were looking rather cross at the sign on the bakery window that announced it would be closed for the holiday. Bruiser was checking his map when Hettie and Tilly reached him, dressed in his leathers and goggles to keep out the cold. The Butters' Morris Minor Convertible was parked behind Miss Scarlet with its windscreen steamed up. Betty, who had elected to drive, was revving the engine as her sister attempted to clear the windscreen with her paw. Both cats were wearing heavy coats and together they filled the front of the vehicle.

Hettie waved a greeting and was thankful that she and Tilly had the luxury of travelling in Miss Scarlet's sidecar. The Morris had a bit of a reputation for pleasing itself: it regularly boiled over when least expected, transformed itself into an open top car on rainy days and backfired at the least opportunity. Tilly glanced across at the post office, noticing that Lavender Stamp's curtains were drawn in her upstairs windows. She felt sad for the postmistress, whom no one really liked, and wondered what sort of Christmas she would be having behind those closed curtains.

Bruiser took charge of the tartan shopper and put it into the boot of the Morris as Hettie and Tilly clambered into the sidecar and pulled the lid shut. With a nod to the Butters, he leapt up onto the motorbike, kicked it into life and headed out of the town in the direction of the Much-Purrings. The Morris had a slightly rougher getaway, on account of Betty forgetting to release the handbrake. The car responded by jerking its way up the high street, backfiring as it went, until Beryl released the brake and left her sister to concentrate on steering.

As predicted, the Much-Purring villages had pulled all the stops out for the season. The village pond in Much-Purring-on-the-Rug was a picture. 'Ooh look,' said Tilly, as Bruiser slowed down to take in the scene, 'they've built a barge for Santa and his elves. Don't they look jolly? And look at that huge tree on the village green – it's much bigger than the one outside Malkin and Sprinkle.'

'Well, that's because this is where all the rich cats live,' Hettie pointed out. 'Mostly retired, living in perfect cottages with nothing to do but preen their gardens and attend parish council meetings. I bet they planned that barge last Christmas and spent all year building it, but it does look fantastic.'

The next village along was not so pleasing as far as Hettie was concerned. Much-Purring-on-the-Blanket had gone for a more religious theme, featuring the entire nativity scene on the green, with light-up camels for the three kings and a revolving stable tableau. 'Looks like one of Verity Sinkton's efforts,' said Hettie. 'Shabby and tacky and that Virgin Mary has seen better days. Why they trust Verity to put on the display every year I'll never understand – she's got her claw into everything in this village, as well as her column in the *Daily Snout*.'

'Just because she's married to the vicar doesn't make her a bad cat,' Tilly pointed out, as Bruiser increased his speed and left the village behind. 'You don't like her because she's religious.'

'Well, you're right there. If she kept it to herself I wouldn't mind, but all that pious nonsense she serves up in her column, telling us how to live our lives, doesn't sit well with me, especially when she follows it up with light-up camels. Last week's article was all about how we should shun the idea of treats at Christmas and put the money we spend on them in the church's collection plate on Christmas Day, yet she was busily buying up everything she could get her paws on in the festive section of the food hall the other day while I was queuing at the pre-packed meat counter. It's total hypocrisy.'

'I see what you mean,' said Tilly, pulling their tartan rug up to her chin as the first snowflakes began to fall.

The countryside began to change dramatically from well-kept villages to wide open fenland as they reached Scratchers Cross. The road was long and straight, with ditches on either side which added to the bleakness, punctuated only occasionally by a distant farmhouse. The black soil that Bruiser had mentioned was gradually turning white, giving some relief to the monotonous landscape. The snow was now coming thick and fast and settling on the road. Bruiser slowed to a more careful speed as he approached a humpbacked bridge; Miss Scarlet negotiated it successfully but the Morris stalled before reaching the top and slid back down again. Betty responded by restarting the engine and slamming her foot down hard on the accelerator, gaining the top of the bridge at speed before killing the engine and allowing the Morris to coast down the other side. Bruiser breathed a sigh of relief as they continued, hoping that they would reach their destination before the route became impassable.

The road signs were few and far between and the droves that led off the main road were little more than dirt tracks, now completely covered in snow. A sign loomed before them, announcing that they had reached Dead Bones Dyke and the small convoy pressed on for mile after mile as the snow began to pile up in drifts at the side of the road. Eventually another signpost showed up ahead of them, but it was unreadable. Bruiser signalled for the Morris to stop and cut the engine on Miss Scarlet. Getting off the bike, he waded through the snow and cleared the sign with his paw, establishing that they had reached Gallows Edge Drove; according to his map, The Fishgutter's Arms was only a mile down the road. Betty had had the sense to keep the engine running on the Morris but Miss Scarlet took several kicks before she eventually responded, much to the relief of Bruiser, Hettie and Tilly.

If they hadn't been looking for it, they might have missed their destination altogether. It was Hettie who saw it first and threw the lid back on the sidecar to let Bruiser know. The inn was set back from the road and looked unwelcoming, with no lights from its windows; in fact, to Hettie's eyes it looked completely derelict. There was no smoke coming from its chimneys, the windows looked vacant with no sign of life within and not the slightest hint of Christmas cheer. Bruiser turned the bike off the road, bringing it to a standstill outside the building.

'Bloody marvellous!' said Hettie, leaping out of the sidecar, followed by Tilly who looked more than a little upset. Bruiser followed them to the door of the building and it was clear as soon as they reached it that it hadn't been opened for some time. The snow had piled up on the step and there were nailed planks of wood barring the door.

'This don't look good,' said Bruiser, peering through one of the windows. 'It's all dark in there. Looks like no one's been 'ere fer years. I s'pose this *is* the right place?'

'Well, according to that rusty old sign up there it is,' said Hettie, 'but why it's called The Fishgutter's Arms I'll never know – it's miles from the sea. In fact, it's miles from anything. This whole going away for Christmas is turning into a complete nightmare.'

The Butters sat tight in the Morris with the engine still running, waiting for news as Hettie, Tilly and Bruiser circled the inn to see if there was any sign of life. They located two back doors, both barred in the same way as the front, and the windows at the back had been boarded up. By the time they returned to the front of the building, the Morris was turning into a giant snowball and Miss Scarlet could barely be seen at all.

'This is all gettin' serious,' said Bruiser. 'We need ta get some shelter or we'll all freeze ta death. I'm goin' ta 'ave a go at breakin' in.' He waded through the snow to Miss Scarlet and spent some time clearing it away with his paws, trying to open the boot. Eventually he managed to get at his toolbox and set about the planks of wood on the front door. The wood was rotten and didn't need much persuading; the door gave first time as Bruiser put his shoulder to it. Once inside, Hettie, Tilly and Bruiser looked back at the Morris, encouraging the Butters to join them. Beryl flung open the passenger door as Betty switched off the engine and hauled herself out of the driver's seat, sliding round to join her sister as they both pushed the passenger seat forward.

What happened next would be etched on Hettie's memory until the end of time. The two sisters stood by the open car door to help a passenger out of the back seat. 'I just don't believe what I'm seeing,' hissed Hettie. 'They've brought Lavender Stamp with them! Happy bloody Christmas!'

Chapter Four
The Fishgutter's Arms

The Fishgutter's had seen better days and those days seemed a very long time ago as the six cats made their way gingerly into the main bar, which was dominated by a large inglenook fireplace. The dust on the tables and chairs was inches thick and everything smelt of damp. 'It's colder in here than it is outside,' said Tilly, pulling the hood up on her cardigan.

Betty stood shaking her head and running a paw across the dust on one of the tables. 'I just don't understand what's happened. The cat I spoke to last week on the phone – Scampi, I think her name was – said she was looking forward to seeing us. The Christmas Eve dinner was being served at seven, so she was expecting us before then.'

'Well, it's beginning to sound like a con trick,' said Hettie. 'There's no chance of a dinner or anything else in this place. We may as well get back on the road and head for home.'

'No chance of that,' said Bruiser, cleaning the filth off one of the front windows. 'We can't go anywhere in this weather. Snow's comin' down thicker than before an' I can't even see the road any more. Looks like we'll 'ave ta make the best of it.'

'Make the best of it!' said Lavender, who'd been aggressively brushing the snow from her coat and quietly seething until now. 'How exactly do you expect us to do that? Miles from civilisation, trapped in a snowstorm, freezing to death in a building straight out of the nineteenth century!'

Hettie, who had no time for Lavender Stamp and despised everything she stood for, found herself agreeing with every word the postmistress spoke, although she would never own up to this brief and fleeting moment of solidarity.

'There's plenty of logs by that fireplace,' said Bruiser, ignoring Lavender's comments. 'The first thing we 'ave ta do is get this place warmed up.'

'Good thinking,' said Beryl. 'While you get us a fire going, the rest of us will give this place a bit of a clean-up. As our mother used to say, a bit of dust never hurt.'

Hettie and Bruiser set about laying a fire. Tilly went behind the bar to see if she could find anything useful and emerged minutes later, covered in cobwebs, with a tin box full of candles, some old empty bottles to put them in and an ancient box of matches. 'There's lots more things behind the bar,' she said. 'Old tankards and a barrel that says brandy on it.'

Bruiser was grateful for the matches but the box was so damp that they wouldn't strike. 'We needs somethin' ta get this fire goin'. Them logs is too big to start on their own.'

Hettie foraged behind the bar and produced a selection of rather grubby yellowed newspapers. 'These might do,' she said. 'At least they're dry.'

There were only three matches left and Bruiser decided to chance his luck by striking one of them on the bricks in the inglenook. The head of the first match snapped off, but the second produced a flame. He reached for an oily rag out of his toolbox and set it alight, forcing it under one of the logs in the fireplace and adding several of Hettie's screwed up newspapers around it. Tilly joined in by lighting one of the candles from the flames to ensure that they had a constant source of fire in case the first attempt to light the logs failed. Bruiser's oily rag, Hettie's old newspapers and Tilly's matches did the trick: the logs were damp and smoked to start with, giving off an acrid smell, but gradually as the heat got through to them flames began to appear. Bruiser added some smaller logs and built up the fire until it started to give off some heat and Betty and Beryl dragged some of the chairs they'd cleaned over to the inglenook for them all to sit on. Lavender took the one that looked most comfortable, clutching a small valise that she refused to be parted from, and stared into the fire, silently twitching her whiskers and pulling her coat much tighter around her. Tilly lit several more candles and forced them into the bottles she'd found.

It could never be described as a merry scene: even Bob Scratchet might have been disappointed and Scrooge would have been delighted with the frugality of the situation, but with candlelight and everyone managing to warm their paws by the fire their predicament began to improve.

Beryl suddenly leapt to her feet, almost knocking Tilly off the chair next to her. 'What about the hamper, sister?' she exclaimed, as all eyes turned in her direction. 'It's on the back seat of the Morris!'

'Oh my goodness!' said Betty. 'So it is! Mother's advice paid off this time – she always said never go on a journey without a tin of salmon and a pie in your pocket.'

'What a ridiculous thing to say,' said Lavender, missing the point.

'Are you telling us that you've brought a hamper of food with you?' asked Hettie, getting to her feet.

'Yes I am,' said Betty. 'We thought we'd pack a few Christmas treats in case the food wasn't up to much.'

Hettie and Bruiser didn't wait for any further conversation and both headed for the front door. 'If you can get to my tartan shopper, I've got some treats in there too,' Tilly shouted after them.

The two cats were met with blizzard conditions as they threw the door open. Miss Scarlet and the Morris had almost disappeared under the snow. Bruiser picked up one of the rotten planks of wood he'd freed from the door and began clearing a path towards the Butters' car. The snow was fresh and cleared easily but getting into the Morris proved to be much more difficult. Together,

Hettie and Bruiser set about digging the car out of its snowy overcoat with their paws until eventually the passenger door opened, throwing them both onto their backs. Dusting themselves off, they dragged the hamper off the back seat. Hettie slid it up the path back to the inn as Bruiser set about opening the boot of the car to retrieve Tilly's tartan shopper. It took him some time and Tilly watched anxiously from one of the windows, but he eventually triumphed and returned to thaw his paws out.

Hettie had placed the hamper in front of the fire and the six cats stared at it in anticipation before allowing Betty the honour of opening it. The two sisters had packed it together, so there were no surprises for them, but as Betty undid the straps and lifted the lid even Lavender Stamp was heard to utter a grunt of approval, mainly because the first thing she saw was a bottle of sherry.

'I think we should let Tilly loose on the contents as she loves her lists,' said Beryl, kicking off her galoshes and warming her feet.

Tilly didn't need asking twice and set about unpacking the hamper, announcing each item as she went. 'There's a very large pork pie, a roast chicken, a bag of cooked sausages, a box of cheese straws, and sausage rolls, half an Edam cheese, some crusty cobs, two tins of salmon, a tinned ham, a jar of pickled onions, lots of mince pies, a wedge of fruit cake, a bottle of sherry, a tin opener and a bread knife.'

'That's a Christmas feast if ever there was one,' said Hettie. 'I can't believe what I'm seeing. You two have just worked a Christmas miracle.'

Betty and Beryl beamed with satisfaction. They were both feeling guilty about allowing themselves to be duped over the Christmas reservations but now everyone was warm and soon to be well fed, they intended to try and enjoy themselves.

'Before we eat, I think we should take a look around this place,' suggested Hettie. 'We need to make sure we're safe here for the night and try and make ourselves as comfortable as possible. It doesn't look like anyone's been here for years but there may be squatters or animals sheltering.'

'Marvellous!' snapped Lavender. 'So you're suggesting we may all be murdered in our beds in this godforsaken apology for an inn.'

'Not really,' said Hettie, trying to keep the sarcasm out of her voice. 'For a start, we don't seem to have beds to be murdered in and the gods are clearly on our side as they have delivered fire to keep us warm and food to keep us fed. To be honest, we've nothing to complain about compared with lots of cats who are starving out in the cold.' She shared a knowing look with Tilly while Lavender sat stony-faced, staring into the fire with half an eye on the bottle of sherry.

The Butter sisters had always been sympathetic towards Lavender Stamp. They felt sorry for her because she had no friends, no life outside the post office and no wish to engage with any other cat unless she was rebuking them or pointing out their shortcomings. Betty and Beryl had done their best to rescue her from herself by including her in their social round of parties and outings, but she invariably let them down by behaving badly in front of their other friends. The only occasions when the bitterness appeared to fall away were when she had a drink in her paw. 'How about cracking open the sherry?' said Betty diplomatically, getting to her feet. 'It's Christmas Eve after all, so let's see if they have glasses behind this bar.'

'I'll start laying out the supper on one of these tables,' said Beryl. 'Perhaps you'd like to give me a paw, Lavender?'

Grudgingly, Lavender abandoned her bag, leaving it on her seat by the fire. Obviously buoyed up by the prospect of a sherry, she began to pass some of the food from the hamper to Beryl. Hettie and Tilly lit more candles, ready to explore the rest of The Fishgutter's Arms, and Bruiser joined them. Having located a staircase behind a door off the bar, the three cats climbed to the first floor. There was a window on the turn of the stairs which over-looked the back of the inn. The pane was cracked and broken and a small pile of snow was forming on the stair. Tilly shivered as she passed it, not-ing that it was now dark outside and all she could see for miles was a complete white-out. The black fenland soil had been transformed into a magical landscape befitting any Christmas Eve, but the higher up the stairs they went, the more uneasy Tilly became. 'There's a really bad feeling up here,' she said, as the three friends faced a long corri-dor, its floorboards lifting in places and sloping to the right. There were three doors on either side, strangely fitted with heavy iron bolts. 'I think we should go back down to the fire and forget about exploring. It just isn't nice up here.'

'Don't be silly,' said Hettie. 'We need to check the place out. There might even be bedrooms where we can sleep tonight. Those hard old chairs in the bar aren't exactly comfortable.'

'I'll wait out here in the hallway,' said Tilly, trying to stop her teeth chattering. 'I hate opening doors if I don't know what's on the other side of them, especially if they're bolted from the outside.'

Bruiser shot one of the bolts across and opened the first door, which creaked on its rusty hinges. 'Looks really small in 'ere,' he said, raising his candle and casting it around the room. 'Nothin' but a single bed, an old chair an' no window, but there is a blanket an' a pillow of sorts. It must be above the bar, as it's almost warm.'

Hettie tried the next door along. It was stuck, but gave way eventually. 'This room is really small, too, but it also has a bed with a blanket and there is a window. It's barred, though – more like a cell than a bedroom, but it's not cold in here either.'

There were six rooms in total and Hettie and Bruiser opened the doors on all of them. 'Judging by how small they are, I would think that The Fishgutter's Arms was a roadside travellers' inn in its heyday, with cats using it as an overnight stop-off,' suggested Hettie, 'but as the rooms have beds and blankets, I see no reason why we shouldn't sleep in them tonight.'

Tilly could think of several reasons. Having attended a number of séances, she was in no doubt that ghosts existed and her sixth sense was causing her tabby fur to stand on end in the corridor; she was keen to get back to the fire downstairs in the bar.

The atmosphere there was much more convivial when they returned. Lavender Stamp was humming a medley of off-key carols, clutching her third glass of sherry, and Betty and Beryl had created a wonderful table of treats from the hamper.

'The good news is we have bedrooms and blankets,' said Hettie, warming her paws, 'and the rooms are above the bar so they're not even cold. If we build this fire up before we go to bed, we should be warm and comfortable.'

'That is good news,' said Betty, cutting up the pork pie with the bread knife. 'I just can't understand what's gone wrong. I sent the cheque off at the end of November and it was clear that the cat I spoke to on the phone was expecting us. I booked four-star rooms with all mod cons, and put us all down for the full breakfasts rather than those continental offerings.'

'No cat should be asked to start their day with a pastry and a bit of jam,' added Beryl, as she opened a tin of salmon. 'No wonder those continental cats on the TV are so pasty looking. The

French have got a lot to answer for, although I do like a nice fresh baguette with a slice of ham.'

'I was once abandoned on top of the Eiffel Tower during a school trip and had to be rescued by a cat wearing a string of onions and reeking of garlic,' said Lavender, offering her empty glass to Betty for a refill. 'Then we were taken to the Louvre to view the Mona Lisa. That was the day I realised I needed glasses, as you could hardly see her and her self-satisfied grin. I've sold stamps bigger than that painting. Goodness knows what all the fuss is about.'

Hettie was tempted to enquire as to why she'd been abandoned, although if the young Lavender was as cantankerous as the older one the reason was obvious; instead, she helped herself to a large slice of pork pie and resumed her seat by the fire, leaving Betty and Beryl to reminisce about their visit to Paris.

'Sister and I signed up for one of them Gordon Blue cookery courses, where they stick red wine in everything,' said Betty. 'It was just off the Rue Morgue we had to go. Didn't really get much further than qualifying for our aprons before the cat who was running it scalded his paw while he was bain-marieing a lump of chocolate. D'Artagnan

Swill his name was – had to be rushed home in bandages.'

'We didn't mind though,' added Beryl. 'We went shopping instead and spent the rest of the day eating cakes in one of them patisseries they have over there – that's French for sweet stuff, I think. Too much cream and puff for my liking. Nothing to match one of our lovely dense Victoria sandwiches – you know you've had a cake when you've had a slice of that.'

'But your cream horns are lovely,' said Tilly. 'I suppose they might be a bit French. They're my favourites.'

'Bless you,' said Betty. 'That recipe came from our mother, passed down from her mother, so our cream horns are from Lancashire, same as the hot pots.'

All the talk of food had given the six cats a real appetite and for the next hour the main subject of conversation was praise for the contents of the Butters' hamper accompanied by contented grunts of satisfaction. Hettie, now full to bursting, settled back in her chair and lit her catnip pipe, which she'd discovered in Tilly's shopper, blowing smoke rings up the chimney. She cast an eye about the scene before her: with the exception of Lavender Stamp, who was now snoring noisily and still clutching her sherry glass in both paws, she realised that she was surrounded by the cats she most cared for in all the world. In spite of the disappointment over the state of their holiday accommodation, this Christmas Eve was turning into something quite special. It was as if they'd all stepped back in time to a simpler life, lit by candles and warmed by trees cut down from an ancient forest. The bar at The Fishgutter's Arms had come to life, offering shelter to its weary travellers as the snowstorm still raged across the fen. They were warm and well fed, which – in the scheme of things – was all that really mattered. The magic of the season swirled around them as they dozed by the fire – but they were not alone, as they were all soon to discover.

Chapter Five
Midnight Approaches

Hettie woke with a start as one of the logs tumbled out of the grate, throwing up a cascade of sparks. Bruiser responded by pitching it back into the fire with the tongs he'd found on the settle. 'What time is it?' she asked, noticing that all the candles they'd lit had burnt down to stubs.

Bruiser threw a couple of large logs on the fire and checked his pocket watch as everyone began to stir from their uncomfortable dozing positions. 'Quarter ta twelve,' he said, getting out of his chair and stretching his legs. He crossed to the window where the snow had drifted, obscuring half the pane. 'It's still comin' down a bit and I can't even see where Miss Scarlet and the Morris is parked. We're goin' ta 'ave to dig 'em out in the mornin'.'

'Not exactly the Christmas I'd planned for us,' said Betty.

'Quite,' snapped Lavender, officiously cleaning her spectacles on the corner of her cardigan.

Beryl yawned and poked a stray sausage roll into her mouth. 'Perhaps we'll stay at home next year, sister, or take one of those cruises to somewhere hot.'

The thought of spending Christmas on a cruise ship with Lavender Stamp didn't appeal to Hettie, but she said nothing.

'Did you say a quarter to twelve?' asked Tilly excitedly. 'That means it's almost Christmas! We should all be in our beds by midnight or Christmas might not come at all.'

'I think we should use those rooms upstairs,' suggested Hettie. 'These hard old chairs aren't the most comfortable things to spend the night on.'

'I'll second that,' said Betty, stretching. 'My lumbago is playing up a treat. I'll be good for nothing if I have to spend the night on this chair, so show me a bed and I'll happily collapse on it.'

'And my head is thumping,' piped up Lavender, forcing her spectacles back onto her head. 'I think it's all that smoke from the fire. I'd appreciate a lie down and perhaps a small sherry to take up with me?'

The rest of the cats shared a look, all painfully aware of why Lavender had a headache. The empty sherry bottle next to her chair was testament to that. 'You'll have to make do with a nip of brandy from behind the bar,' said Beryl, 'although personally I'd prefer a hot milky drink, but I don't see how that's to be achieved.'

Now that a hot milky drink had been mentioned, everyone looked crestfallen except Lavender, who tottered off her chair and made unsteady progress towards the bar, disappearing behind it as she grappled with the keg of brandy. Mercifully, the contents were long gone and she emerged hissing insults at no one in particular and grabbed her overnight bag from the chair.

Tilly set new candles in the bottles, lit them from the fire and passed them round so that everyone had one to take upstairs. She could see the sense in using the beds, although she was still uneasy about the atmosphere in the corridor above. They all made their way up the stairs, careful to avoid the pile of snow that had blown in from the broken window. 'Take your pick,' said

Hettie. 'All the rooms are pretty basic but beggars can't be choosers.'

Tilly, who had strong reservations about being upstairs at all, chose the first room on the right of the corridor. Hettie chose the one next door and Bruiser let himself in to the final room on that side, leaving the three rooms opposite for Betty, Beryl and Lavender...

Parcel 'em up,
And float 'em nice.
Old Mrs Smith,
Has paid the price!

Tilly closed the door behind her and lodged her candle on the windowsill next to the bed. She was pleased to have a room with a window. She could hear the distant chime of church bells and, looking out through the bars, she witnessed an extraordinary sight: far across the fen a procession of cats was moving slowly in a long line, all black against the snow like cut-out shadows of themselves, punctuated occasionally by twinkling lanterns. She turned back to the bed and froze.

The cat sat in the corner of the room, only a matter of feet from where Tilly was standing, and as Tilly looked at her the room became icy and the warmth from the downstairs fire drained away. She wanted to cry out, but a lump constricted her throat as the visitor stared back at her. 'Don't you mind me,' the cat said. 'I can't hurt you. My time has passed these hundred years. I'm only fit to wander now, as there's no peace to be had after what I've done.'

Tilly fought desperately to find her voice and when she did it was surprisingly calm and matter-of-fact. 'What did you do?' she asked, fearful of the reply.

'I'm Mrs Smith, the Kitten Killer. Pleased to make your acquaintance, I'm sure.'

'How many kittens?' Tilly found herself asking, although she didn't really want to know the answer.

'Too many to count on me claws, but enough to get me hanged. I thought I was providing a service, see – some folks would have put them in a sack and thrown them in a ditch, but I helped them on their way by smothering as I sang to them. Dear little things, a little wriggle and they was gone.'

'But why did you kill them?'

''Cause I got sixpence for each of them. Bought me a nice tot of gin or two and paid for me lodgings.'

'Why did they have to die?'

''Cause there was too many mouths to feed and it was kinder than turning them out to starve, poor little things. After I'd done for them, I'd parcel them up and float them down the river to give them a nice send-off, but that was me undoing.'

'Why? What happened?'

'I got caught by an old cat living on a barge. He'd been fishing me parcels out of the river for weeks, trying to catch me out. That night I had six parcels and he was waiting for me. Caught red-pawed, I was.'

'But why are you here in this room, tonight of all nights?' asked Tilly, becoming bolder by the second. 'I don't understand why you are haunting me.'

'Well, that's 'cause you're in my room, so you're really haunting me. I lays me head down every Christmas Eve in this room, waiting to meet me maker at the Christmas Day hangings at Gallows Edge at the pleasure of Ruben Catcraft, the hanging cat of the fens. Folks come from all over to watch. I went meself once and it was the best Christmas Day I ever had – gin flowing like water, kept the frost away. We went skating across the fen after and had a merry old time of it.'

Tilly moved closer to the cat, hoping that she might just disappear; instead, she was able to take in every inch of her. Mrs Smith was a short-haired brown cat, dressed in a full length, dull grey dress, the skirt patched in several places, and a blue shawl thrown about her shoulders. The grey bonnet on her head was untied and perched at a jaunty angle, as if she'd only just thrown it on. Her feet were bare and covered in sores. 'Aren't you frightened about what will happen to you tomorrow?'

Mrs Smith shook her head and smiled. 'Not any more,' she said.

Tilly was suddenly aware that the bells had stopped tolling. She turned briefly to the window and when she turned back Mrs Smith was gone.

High kicks and petticoats,
Never so humble.
Gents beware of
Millicent Rumble.

Lavender Stamp was unaccustomed to anyone sitting on her bed, so when Millicent Rumble the Music Hall Murderer decided to rest her dead bones on the bed in the room Lavender had chosen, it came as a bit of a shock. Millicent sat down on the stroke of midnight and Lavender sat up, still hugging her overnight bag to her. In Lavender's world there were no such things as ghosts, so she treated her intruder like any other interloper into her personal space.

Her headache persisted, which made her even more short-tempered than usual, and she didn't mince her words as she addressed her visitor. 'And who, may I ask, are you? And what do you mean by bursting into my room and having the audacity to sit on my bed dressed in that ridiculous outfit?'

There was no doubt that Millicent Rumble had dressed to kill. As one of the most formidable music hall stars of her day, appearance was everything: the bright red bodice and full skirt – stiffened with a froth of petticoats and embellished with a hat sporting a white ostrich feather – was her customary wear as she played to the balcony and twitched her delicate whiskers at the well-heeled gentlemen cats in the boxes. The outfit now looked past its best, stained and torn in places, just like Millicent.

'Sorry to bother you, deary, but that's my bed you're sleeping in,' said Millicent, not in the slightest bit intimidated by the postmistress. 'You surely wouldn't begrudge me a peaceful night's sleep before my final performance tomorrow, would you?'

'I'm sure I don't know what you mean,' said Lavender, preparing to turn her back on the stranger and settle down in the blanket. 'This room is taken and I'd have thought that was obvious. Now kindly leave me in peace and shut the door behind you – it's getting cold in here.'

'Well I never!' said Millicent. 'I'd call that just plain rude. You want to watch yourself. It's a good job I've passed on or I could be tempted to send you on your way like some of my gentlemen. They thought they could get the better of me, but they went to their graves before I did.'

Lavender sat up again. The pain in her head was getting worse and for the first time in her life she was seriously considering giving up sherry altogether. 'This is clearly some fancy dress theatrical experience you're putting me through,' she said. 'I've no idea who booked you, but your thespian antics are not welcome and all this talk of gentlemen going to their graves is rather a bad script – and a tawdry one at that. Am I supposed to believe that you're some sort of femme fatale, dressed as you are? I might tell you that there will be no Oscars for you. I suggest you reconsider your profession before it gets you into serious trouble.'

Millicent threw her head back and laughed. 'It's a bit late for that, deary. Try telling that to the judge and his black cap – no mercy there. I was on a good run until that backstage boy caught me entertaining one of those gentlemen cats with a knife. Slit his throat from ear to ear, I did, and took his wallet. The boy ran before I could catch him and I was done for. Dragged away before the second half of my show. I thought if I owned up to the others they'd go lightly on me but when I told the detective that I'd killed four more it just seemed to make things worse.'

Lavender was beginning to feel uneasy, questioning exactly what or who was sitting on her bed. She wanted to blame the drink or the passive smoke from Hettie's catnip pipe, but what faced her was no brief hallucination. The creature showed no sign of leaving the room and seemed happy to chat away about her misfortunes, as if Lavender herself had entered and was taking part in a weird sort of play. Taking a more practical approach with her visitor, she decided to ask the questions. 'Am I to believe that you have actually murdered five gentlemen cats?'

'Six, actually, but I didn't admit to the first one. Not that it matters now how many I finished off.'

'And are you telling me that you were sentenced to death by the old court system?'

'Not sure how old it was, but yes, that's why I'm here in this room, waiting.'

'Waiting for what?' snapped Lavender, losing patience with Millicent's ambiguous answers.

'Waiting for Ruben Catcraft to fetch me in the morning.'

'Well, at least you'll have a lift home, although I doubt he'll get through in this weather. Is he part of this theatrical experience, for want of a better word?'

Millicent sniffed and melted away as if she'd never been there.

Jabari Cook,
A handsome cat,
Killed his master,
And that was that!

The room was nothing like the one Betty thought she had booked. She was grateful for the candle that Tilly had given her, as there was no window, although she thought she heard the sound of distant church bells. It was comforting to know that somewhere out on the snowy fen the coming of Christmas Day was being celebrated, perhaps in the cathedral Bruiser had mentioned. The room wasn't cold, but by no means warm either. She put the bottle with the candle in it on the floor and decided to keep all her clothes on, then crept under the blanket on the bed and pulled it up to her chin. Her lumbago was bothering her and she wriggled to find a comfortable position to lie in.

Turning onto her side, she was suddenly aware of a dark shape in the corner of the room. It blinked, revealing two large, bright, round staring eyes that twinkled in the candlelight. Betty's heart began to thump in her chest and she lay very still, hoping that whatever it was would go away, but the eyes continued to stare at her. She tried to rationalise with herself that perhaps a touch of indigestion was the cause of the vision before her; one pickled onion too many perhaps, but the shape moved towards the bed and she could see that it was a large, magnificent black cat.

She shrank into the blanket, fearful of what the cat might do next, but he came no further and put his paws up as if to defend himself. 'Please don't be frightened, Miss, I mean you no harm. I never hurt no one 'cept my master and he was a bad cat.'

'Who are you?' was all Betty could think to say as the cat continued to blink at her in a very disarming way.

'My name is Jabari Cook, Miss. Jabari means brave. I come from Africa and I am most pleased to make your acquaintance.'

Betty took a long look at the cat in front of her before continuing the conversation. He was perhaps the most handsome black cat she'd ever seen – beautiful, in fact. He was dressed in rags and his two front paws were shackled, but his whole demeanour spoke to her and strangely she had no fear of him, although she knew in her heart that he no longer inhabited the world she lived in. 'Africa is a long way away,' she said. 'What brought you here?'

'A slave ship, Miss, in 1875. The ship was captured by the British Navy and all us slaves were freed, but we had no money to make a life here so I became a servant to a rich merchant cat and I worked in his big house as a cook. He gave me my second name and he was a good master but he died and I was sold by his agent at a hiring fair to a bad cat who beat me.'

'Why did he beat you?'

'Because it made him happy, Miss. He had a farm and me and some other cats freed from slavery worked in his fields.'

'So did you hurt him because he beat you?'

'No, Miss. I got used to his beatings; we all did. One day I was called up to the farmhouse to drive the mistress in the cart to market. She was always kind to me and taught me to read and write in secret. I loved my mistress and I would have done anything for her. That day he caught her giving me food from the kitchen and he beat her with his whip. I couldn't just stand and watch, so I took the whip off him and threw him against the cart. I didn't mean for him to die, but he split his head open on one of the wheels. I knew I'd done wrong, but I was just trying to save the mistress. She ran back into the house and that was the last

I saw of her. All the other slaves turned against me and I was hunted down and put in these chains. I begged to be sent back to my homeland, but they sent me here to be hanged on Christmas Day.'

Betty remembered what Bruiser had said about Gallows Edge and the barbaric mass hangings in the fens, and suddenly felt a terrible sadness for the cat in front of her. If he was to be believed, then he had suffered a great injustice – but he had taken a life, and in the days when he had lived there was only one punishment. 'Why do you come back to haunt this place that brought you so much misery?' she asked, trying to understand why he'd appeared to her in the first place. 'Wouldn't you rather your spirit be free to return to Africa, to your homeland?'

'My spirit can never be free of this place. I died here and I am unforgiven. I took a life and I am paying for that. This is my eternity. It is all I have.'

Betty was suddenly aware that the distant bells had fallen silent. She was also surprised to find herself crying. Through the watery mist of her tears, she watched as Jabari Cook receded into the corner of the room, returning to the shadows whence he had come until there was no trace of him left.

Agnes Buckle
Takes delight
In serving stew
That's not quite right!

Beryl Butter would have preferred to share a room with her sister, but the rooms at The Fish-gutter's were barely big enough for one, let alone two well-rounded, middle-aged cats from Lancashire whose passion for food was more than obvious. The room reminded her of the overnight sleeper train that she and Betty had often travelled to Scotland on when they had had enough time on their paws for a proper holiday. These days the bakery took up much of their time and they were both aware of how much the cats in the town had come to rely on them. When Betty had suggested they go away for Christmas to be waited on paw and foot, Beryl had jumped at the idea, and including Hettie, Tilly and Bruiser in the party meant that they would be spending Christmas with the cats they cared about most. Including Lavender Stamp arose more from a sympathetic duty than a wish to spend time with her. In past years they'd invited her to join them for Christmas lunch, as it was the only offer she was likely to get. Betty had been convinced that Lavender would refuse their offer of a break at The Fishgutter's but the half-hearted invitation had rather backfired.

This Christmas was meant to be special, a holiday of luxury and good cheer but, as Beryl sat on the single bed clutching her lighted candle, she wondered what had gone wrong. There was nothing luxurious about the place they found themselves in. The candle, as if it sensed her melancholy, spluttered and went out, leaving her in complete darkness. She abandoned it on the floor and felt for the blanket, pulling it off the bed and wrapping it around her shoulders. She was just considering whether to join her sister after all when she was suddenly aware of a presence in the room. Instantly she thought of rats, but there was no scuffling and she rubbed her eyes with her paws to accustom them to the darkness.

To her surprise and horror, the candle she'd abandoned reignited and rose up as if carried across the room to a chair by the door. The flame cast an eerie glow upon the bodiless head of an elderly female cat whose face moved and contorted in the flickering light. Beryl wanted to cry out but the apparition put a long, curled black claw to its mouth, signalling that she should stay silent.

The face began to grow a body, dressed in black bombazine with a filthy apron that had at some stage been white. Beryl held her breath and closed her eyes, hoping that when she opened them again the cat would have left her in peace; instead the creature spoke, making it clear that she was going nowhere.

'So, what 'ave we gots 'ere?' she rasped in a voice that cut through the gloom like a knife, sharp, brittle and toneless. 'I'm not allowed no visitors, case I murders 'em. I'm not fit ta breathe the same air, see, as civilised folk, but I'll be remembered for me killin's. Agnes Buckle the Workhouse Poisoner, that's what them street criers shouted as I was taken down. What I wants ta know is who are you an' what 'ave you done ta gets yerself a place at the Christmas 'angin's?'

'I haven't done anything,' whispered Beryl, too frightened to raise her voice. 'We're sheltering here from the snowstorm. My sister is in the room next door and we're here with four other friends to spend Christmas.'

'Well, that's a fancy story! Try tellin' that ta Ruben Catcraft when 'e comes ta measure yer neck. There'll be no shelter out on the fen when they strings you up tomorrow. Come on, best ta tell me what you done. I likes ta know who I'm sharin' with.'

Beryl struggled to her feet, deciding to make a run for the door, but Agnes hissed at her. 'No point tryin' ta' escape. E's shot the bolt across. Why don't we pass the time swappin' killin's? I likes ta talk about me killin's.'

Beryl slumped back down on the bed and tried to remember what Irene Peggledrip had said about malevolent spirits at one of the psychic sessions she'd attended. Her general advice seemed to have been to engage with them and agree with anything that was said until the spirit got bored and disappeared. With Agnes Buckle staring at her, the psychic's words seemed easier said than done but Beryl was willing to give it a try.

'So tell me who you've killed, then, if you like,' said Beryl, shivering now and not just with cold, 'but first tell me why you were in the workhouse.'

'I was sent fer not payin' me debts, but most of them cats in there was what they calls imbecility of mind. Violent, screamin' lunatics they were, and they expected me ta live with 'em. I says to meself – Agnes, you needs ta get yerself out before one of 'em cuts yer throat. So I bides me time an' gets me a place in the kitchins servin' dinners. I takes some fly papers an soaks 'em in water and I waits till the old cook's not watchin' an pours me water into the stew. Them lunatics dropped like flies, foamin' at their mouths. I gave 'em somthin' ta scream about. Seven dead in one sittin'. The old cook said the meat was off, but I knew different.'

'So you murdered seven cats in the workhouse by poisoning their food with arsenic just because they were mentally ill?'

Agnes cackled at Beryl's description of her crimes, shaking her head. 'That's a pretty way of puttin' it, but they was lost souls in service to the Devil 'imself. I done them a favour.'

Beryl had once read a book on the barbaric way that inmates were treated in Victorian workhouses, so many of them branded insane for no reason at all – and here it was in reality. 'If the cook thought the meat was off in the stew, how did you get caught?' she asked, becoming genuinely interested in the bizarre story.

Agnes cackled again. 'We 'ad a load more lunatics come from one of them London bedlam places. Really bad, they was, so I gets me fly papers soakin' an' pours it in the gruel pot, but that old cook was watchin' this time an' told 'er suspicions to the workhouse matron. By the time she'd got to me, I'd served the gruel an' three more lunatics was added to me total. I did fer the cook before they locked me away, too – cut 'er 'ead clean off with 'er meat cleaver. She won't be tellin' any more tales. Matron said 'angin' was too good fer me an' I should be drawn an' quartered as well, but I've booked me place in Coffins Dyke.'

'What on earth is Coffins Dyke?'

'It's where they lays us after the 'angin'. When we rots, they spreads us on the fields – good fer the celery. I 'ates the stuff on account of 'avin' no teeth.'

Beryl was beginning to believe that she was trapped in some sort of nightmare. She couldn't decide whether to laugh hysterically or cry out for help. The more Agnes Buckle spoke, the more horrifying the situation became. The candle that Agnes had been clutching spluttered again and went out, plunging the room into darkness. Beryl stiffened, wondering what would happen next. Would the creature pounce, adding to her total of victims? Beryl waited several moments before getting to her feet and crossing to the door.

Salem Jack
Took up his gun,
Fired once
And he was done!

Bruiser was more than used to laying his head down in uncomfortable places. During his years of wandering the highways and byways he'd slept in ditches, barns and had even built himself a makeshift igloo one particularly cold winter's night. Since he'd enjoyed the comfort of his own cosy shed at the bottom of the Butters' garden he'd become soft in his older years. The bed that now faced him at The Fishgutter's Arms was far from comfortable. It was hard on his old bones and the blanket smelt of mould and decay. He was beginning to wish he'd stayed by the fire but he was good at making the best of things. He placed his candle on the floor next to the bed, deciding not to blow it out, and burrowed into the blanket, pulling it tightly around him and closing his eyes.

In the distance he was aware of bells chiming only a few miles down the fen road in the giant cathedral, announcing the midnight mass which would herald in Christmas for those cats who'd trudged through the snow. Sleep came quickly to him as the cares of the day were finally put to bed. He was a cat who thrived on solving problems, handy with his paws and a surprisingly deep thinker, with a thirst for knowledge way beyond the practicalities of his own life. Working for Hettie and Tilly's detective agency suited him very well and, even if the bed was cold and hard, being included in their adventures brought him a great deal of joy.

At first he thought he was dreaming when the hissing began. It took him a moment to realise that the noise wasn't coming from his own throat. He opened his eyes to see a cat's head, its mouth wide open to reveal fangs that dripped with saliva. The creature gave a guttural hiss and Bruiser reacted immediately, throwing off the blanket and leaping on the intruder. The cat was too quick for him and Bruiser fell to the floor. The cat rose up in front of him, its claws fully extended ready to pounce; Bruiser rolled away from the danger and countered the attack by headbutting the creature, but it was as if he'd reacted to thin air. Again the cat came at him hissing and spitting, its eyes bulging from its head, red and angry like pools of fire. It was several seconds before Bruiser realised that, in spite of the creature hitting out at him, he'd felt no blows. Even the saliva dripping from the cat's mouth had made no impression. Bruiser would later say that it was like fighting with an aggressive shadow.

His hackles were up as the creature danced around him and he gave chase across the small room, swiping at it with his paws until he was exhausted. Eventually he sat back on the bed and his tormentor leapt up onto the windowsill above, crouching in the recess and poised to continue his attack. But by now Bruiser had realised that the creature before him was no longer of this world; other than scaring him, it could do no real harm. He decided to take a rational approach to his unwanted visitor and try for a sensible conversation. 'No point 'avin' a go at me,' he began. 'I can see yer angry but it would be good to know who you are an' if I can 'elp in any way.'

The cat blinked and when he opened his eyes again the redness had gone, replaced by a sharp, striking green that shone in the candlelight. His face softened and he began to lick one of his paws nervously before responding. 'I'm Jack Hawks, or I was once. I'm not sure who I am now or even if I'm anything at all. They used to call me Salem Jack, but that was a very long time ago – before, before…' The cat tailed off, seeming to forget what he was going to say.

Relieved to have established some kind of dialogue, Bruiser decided to introduce himself. 'My name is Bruiser an' I'm stayin' 'ere with some friends cos we're snowed in till mornin'.'

Salem Jack twisted round to look out of the window and turned back to Bruiser, shaking his head. 'There's no snow out there, just the Fen Blow lifting the soil.'

Bruiser stood and looked out of the window, astonished to see that there *was* no snow, just a dust storm spiralling the black fenland soil up into the air like a mass of migrating birds. The wind was audible and howled across the fen, bending the leafless trees in its wake. Bruiser rubbed his eyes and returned to sit on the bed, feeling even more confused.

'You are in my time,' said Jack, 'and while I am here you see what I see.'

'I don't understand,' said Bruiser, now completely unnerved by the situation. 'What is your time?'

'My time is running out,' said Jack. 'If tomorrow comes I will die by the rope and my body will be thrown into Coffins Dyke.'

'So are you part of the mass 'angin's?'

'Yes,' said the cat, jumping down from the windowsill and landing on the bed next to Bruiser. 'I murdered Squire Blacklock for beating my dogs.'

'Isn't that a bit strange, a cat 'avin' dogs?' said Bruiser. 'An' why did 'e beat 'em?'

'I kept his hunting hounds for him. It was my job and I loved those dogs. One day the Squire had been out hunting and the dogs hadn't managed to run the fox they were chasing to ground and it got away. That night, while I was putting them back in their kennels, Blacklock turned up and started beating them with a shovel as a punishment for ruining his day. He killed two of them before I got to him, so I took my gun, shot his head off and fed his body to the dogs. The old cat who was his gamekeeper told on me, so I was done for. But I'm pleased I killed him and the dogs had a good dinner that night.'

'So why are you 'ere at The Fishgutter's?'

'I am here at the pleasure of Her Majesty the Queen and Ruben Catcraft, who sleeps soundly in the room next door.'

'Isn't 'e the famous nineteenth-century 'angin' cat?'

'Oh yes, indeed he is,' said Jack, getting to his feet. 'Only the best for me and the others.'

'What others?' asked Bruiser but Salem Jack didn't reply; he simply disappeared.

And I am as a pendulum,
That swings and never stays.
The death clock of this bad old world,
That cancereth away.

Hettie sat on the bed and shivered. The room she had chosen was cold and damp. There was no window to focus on and certainly no comfort from the rough blanket on the bed. The candle Tilly had given her had gone out as soon as she shut the door behind her. The distant Christmas bells brought her no joy as she sat in the dark, wishing to be anywhere but in this room at The Fishgutter's Arms. As she stared into the darkness she promised herself that she would never agree to leaving home at Christmas again. It was a kind offer from the Butters but right from the start she'd fought against it, and now there would be no Christmas until they had dug themselves out of the nightmare they all found themselves in.

Suddenly her mind was made up: she would go and get Tilly and they would spend the night by the fire in the bar. Even if the chairs were uncomfortable it would be better than this room, which was little more than a prison cell.

She stood up and crossed to the door but as she groped for the handle, her paw was smacked away from it with some force. Confused, she reached for the handle again; this time she was pushed back onto the bed by something she couldn't see but which was very present in the room. She fought to stand but whatever it was was just too strong for her.

The voice, when it came, was terrifying – a low, deep growl that splintered the air as if it was at the other end of a tunnel. 'There's no escaping me,' it said. 'I'll have that pretty neck of yours stretched nicely until your tongue turns blue and your eyes burst out of your head.'

Hettie laughed out loud, thinking that Bruiser was playing a trick on her. 'You gave me a real scare for a minute there,' she said. 'I thought it was a ghost but I'm glad of the company. It's horrible in here. Why can't I see you?'

The voice came again and this time Hettie froze as the form of a thin, grey cat materialised in front of her. 'Now you can see me as I see you,' it said, 'and I promise you that tomorrow will be much more horrible than this room I'm keeping you in tonight.'

Hettie swallowed hard, assessing the danger she was in before confronting her unwanted visitor.

'Who are you?' she snapped, trying to control the situation, 'and why are you here?'

The cat grinned at her and licked his lips as if he'd just enjoyed a good dinner. 'I am Ruben Catcraft, hanging cat to Her Majesty in these parts, in loyal service to our Queen and country.'

'Well someone should have told you that those services are no longer required. They stopped hanging cats a long time ago,' said Hettie, deciding not to put up with any nonsense from what she now accepted was a ghost. Ruben scratched his head with one of his paws, looking slightly confused, then put on a display of guttural hissing, but Hettie would have none of it. 'You can stop that right now,' she said. 'It doesn't frighten me. I am very much alive and you are obviously very dead. For your information, we are in the 1970s, living in a civilised society where there is no capital punishment and no need for hanging cats. We sort out our problems in a very different way from the barbaric laws of the past, so I suggest you stop that ridiculous noise you're making and go back to where you came from.'

Ruben Catcraft looked even more confused by Hettie's onslaught. He was clearly not used to being challenged in any way regarding his chosen profession and much of what Hettie had said was completely beyond his understanding – especially the bit about him being dead. For the hundred years that he had inhabited The Fishgutter's Arms, it had never occurred to him that he was living in a world of spirits; over the years, he'd enjoyed frightening visitors who'd turned up out of curiosity and left as soon as he appeared to them, but the cat in front of him now was different and he found it refreshing to have a proper conversation. 'If what you say is true,' he said, 'then what do you do with murderers if you don't hang them?'

'In my experience,' said Hettie, 'most murderers, once caught, slink off and bring about their own destruction in one way or another. We sometimes have to lock them up and throw away the key, but getting another cat to hang them goes against everything we as a society believe in. There are lots of reasons why cats are driven to killing other cats and all of that has to be taken into consideration. After all, if I understand you correctly, you yourself are a mass murderer. Had it ever occurred to you that some of those cats you've hanged might have been innocent, or might have had a very good reason for killing? Maybe to protect themselves or others from harm?'

'I'm no murderer,' Ruben protested. 'I'm just doing a job and doing it well. It's not up to me to think about whose neck I'm putting my rope around or what they've done to deserve it. It's a real craft, what I do. Some hanging cats botch the job every time, leaving the murderers dangling and choking. Some crowds loves a messy hanging but I pride myself on breaking the necks as soon as I swing them. That's why I do the Christmas Day hangings here at Gallows Edge. Folk come from far and wide to one of my mass hangings because they know they'll get a good day out with humane executions.'

Hettie had a problem with the words 'humane executions' but decided to move on, intrigued now by why Ruben Catcraft was haunting The Fishgutter's Arms in the first place. 'I understand what your job was but why are you still here? Did you die in this place?'

'I'm here to escort five cats to the gallows. Mrs Theodora Smith, Agnes Buckle, Jabari Cook, Millicent Rumble and Jack Hawks, known as Salem Jack.'

'So where are all these murderers?' asked Hettie, looking around the room and half-expecting them to pop up at any moment.

'They're locked away in the other rooms up here, saying their prayers and maybe even writing their confessions – that's if they *can* write. Those confessions fetch a pretty penny for the street sellers if they get their grubby paws on them.'

Hettie was suddenly fearful for her friends in the rooms along the corridor but there was one question Ruben hadn't answered. 'So *did* you die here?' she repeated.

Ruben Catcraft looked directly into Hettie's eyes as if he were staring into her soul. She felt sickness rising in her as flames burst out from the floorboards and consumed the cat in front of her until there was nothing left of him but a scorch mark where he had stood. She rushed to open the door and found Bruiser, Tilly, Betty, Beryl and Lavender Stamp all in the corridor outside their rooms. By the looks on their faces, they had all had visits from unwanted guests. Bruiser checked his pocket watch. It was five minutes past midnight on Christmas Day.

Chapter Six
Sugared Almonds and Nut Brittle

The six cats made their way back down to the bar in silence, as if speaking out loud would make the trauma they had all gone through more real than it needed to be. The warmth of the fire did nothing to take away the chill they all felt and it was Lavender Stamp who broke the silence by having a delayed panic attack. Betty responded by grabbing the paper bag that the mince pies had come in and forcing Lavender to breathe into it. When all was calm again, Hettie decided to take control of the situation.

'It's clear to me that we have walked into some sort of time warp,' she began. 'I assume we've all seen ghosts, judging by the looks on your faces?'

Everyone nodded in agreement. 'The best way to deal with this is to face it head on. Whatever went on in those rooms upstairs may have frightened us, but we've come to no real harm. I suggest that we share our experiences so that we can get a better understanding of what's happening here.'

'Spoken like a true detective,' said Beryl, 'and we've still plenty of food left from the hamper. We could just pretend we're sitting round this lovely fire, eating treats and telling ghost stories. It is Christmas after all.'

'And what if the ghosts decide to come down and join us?' suggested Lavender. 'I just can't see how you can all sit around telling each other stories with goodness knows what upstairs in those rooms. We should get out now, while we still can.'

'No chance of that,' Bruiser pointed out. 'As it is, we'll 'ave ta dig the Morris an' Miss Scarlet out of the snow in the mornin'. If we go out there now we'll freeze ta death.'

'Well, I'm for another slice of pork pie,' said Hettie, diplomatically steering the conversation to nicer things, 'and I wouldn't mind one of those pickled onions to go with it.'

Betty obliged by passing the jar and Tilly added to the feast by mining the nut brittle and sugared almonds from her tartan shopper and passing the Turkish delight to Bruiser. With the exception of Lavender Stamp, who sat sulkily nibbling on a sausage roll, the rest of the cats entered into the spirit of Christmas, sharing food, treats and the details of their recent ghostly encounters around the fire. Eventually Lavender decided to join in and was persuaded to share her encounter with Millicent Rumble as her companions listened with interest.

When all the tales were told it was left to Hettie to attempt to make sense of them. 'What I find curious is the appearance of Ruben Catcraft,' she said, filling her catnip pipe and lighting it. 'All the other ghosts were due to be executed so we know how they died – but not Ruben. And why are they all haunting this place and not out on the fen where they were hanged?'

It was a question no one was willing or able to answer. It had already been a long night and tiredness was setting in. One by one they curled up on their chairs and fell asleep, leaving Hettie to ponder late into the night, keeping a watchful eye in case any of The Fishgutter's unwanted guests decided to put in another appearance. In the early hours, she finally gave in to sleep.

Chapter Seven
Christmas Morning

Bruiser was first to wake and struggled stiffly from his chair to put logs onto the fire, which had burnt down low. He padded to the window and was pleased to see that the snow had stopped falling and the sun had put in an appearance. A strangely deep blue sky presided over the snow-bound countryside and made the terrors of the night before quite unbelievable. Two mountains of white stood out in The Fishgutter's car park and Bruiser sighed, knowing that the first job of the day would be to dig the Morris and the motorbike and sidecar out of their snowy cocoon. He turned back to the fire where Hettie and Tilly were stirring, just in time to see Lavender Stamp fall off her chair as she turned over in her sleep. The three cats came to Lavender's rescue but the commotion woke Betty and Beryl, who both sat up and attempted to rub some life into their limbs.

''Appy Christmas everyone!' said Bruiser brightly. 'Snow's stopped so we could 'ave a go at diggin' ourselves out if you're all up for it?'

'Not before breakfast,' Hettie pointed out, eyeing up the somewhat desecrated remains of Betty and Beryl's hamper. 'Can't shovel snow on an empty stomach, can we?'

'I'd kill for a milky tea,' said Betty. 'All that pastry from last night has made me thirsty.'

'No chance of that round here, sister,' said Beryl. 'You'll have to suck one of Tilly's sugared almonds instead.'

Tilly offered the sweets round and immediately wished she hadn't when a gurgling sound came from Lavender Stamp, who had inadvertently swallowed hers whole and got it stuck in her throat. Hettie was delighted to assist by giving the postmistress a good thumping on the back until the sugared almond broke free of her mouth and shot into the fire.

'That was a close call,' said Betty. 'Not the way to go, choking yourself on Christmas Day on a sugared almond – just imagine that on your tombstone.'

'Reminds me of Carlton Shortbread,' said Beryl. 'Him and his wife Dillys lived next door to us in Lancashire. Dillys loved putting sixpences in her Christmas pudding and any other loose change she found lying about. Carlton set to with his pudding after a roast turkey lunch and choked while Dillys was in the kitchen trying to thaw out the brandy butter. He was dead as a doornail when she came back to the table. Buried him at New Year and vowed she'd only ever eat trifle on Christmas Day from that moment on.'

Lavender was not impressed by Beryl's recollections of a Lancashire Christmas but Hettie, Tilly and Bruiser fell about laughing while Betty doled out the meagre rations left in the hamper.

'Right,' said Bruiser, brushing the pastry from his whiskers with his paw, 'if we don't want ta spend another night 'ere we'd better 'ave all paws to the pump ta get that snow cleared. We'll 'ave ta use anythin' we can find ta get it shifted.'

At the thought of spending another night at The Fishgutter's Arms even Lavender showed willing by equipping herself with two tankards from behind the bar. Betty found an old bucket and Beryl armed herself with a shove halfpenny board. Tilly took the small coal shovel from the fireplace and Hettie and Bruiser chose the planks of wood that Bruiser had pulled from the door when they'd first arrived.

The icy cold air bit at their faces as they emerged from the warmth of the bar and out into the car park. The snow had sculpted the landscape in drifts that any artist would have been proud of and the sun created a blinding light that sparkled and danced before their eyes. Before setting to work with her shovel, Tilly glanced up at the windows of The Fishgutter's and was certain that she saw a pale face at one of them. She shivered as the memory of her encounter with Mrs Smith came back to her but said nothing.

Together, the six cats toiled away, clearing a path from the front door to the Morris. Betty, Beryl and Lavender scrabbled with their paws, gradually removing the snow from the car while Hettie, Tilly and Bruiser set about Miss Scarlet. Eventually both vehicles were clear of the snow.

'We'd better see if they'll start up,' suggested Bruiser, surveying the build-up of snow where the road had been. 'Even if we get the engines started, I'm not sure the road is passable – that's if we can find it. There's ditches on either side an' we wouldn't want ta' end up in one of 'em.'

The hopelessness of their situation suddenly dawned on them and a return to the fire in the bar to thaw out their frozen paws seemed the logical next move – but a Christmas miracle was slowly making its way across the fen, getting louder and louder as it approached. The giant monster made slow but sure progress, gobbling up the snow and shooting it high into the air on either side of the road, growing ever closer to where the six cats stood in awe of the huge machine.

The cat driving the snow plough was wearing a Santa hat and offered a cheerful wave as the machine ground to a halt on the road in front of them. 'Happy Christmas to you,' she said, jumping down. 'You all look frozen to death. Can I help?'

Hettie stepped forward to respond but was pushed out of the way by Betty. 'I just don't believe it!' she said, sliding towards the cat. 'If it isn't Flavia Ashton all the way from Lancashire!'

'Well I never!' the cat replied. 'Fancy meeting up with the Butter sisters after all these years! I'd heard you'd gone south after your ma died but I never expected to see you again.'

'And why are you here?' asked Beryl. 'Who's looking after your farm at Pendle?'

'I sold up and came here a few years back,' explained Flavia. 'Them hills was getting too much and I was offered a celery farm across the fen, so I jumped at it. Nice little business on the flat and that snow plough came with it. I love me tractors, but that beast there is a beauty,' she said, waving her paw in its direction. 'Anyway, what are you all doing out here? Don't tell me you've been in that old place. It's haunted, you know – no one who lives round here goes anywhere near.'

'We did have to spend the night here,' said Betty. 'There's been a mistake over a Christmas booking. I think we must have come to the wrong place in the snowstorm last night. We had no choice but to make the best of it.'

'Bless you, you sound just like your ma – always looked on the bright side, she did. The thing is Scampi Kelynack has been meaning to take that old pub sign down for ages. The whole place needs pulling down. The proper Fishgutter's Arms is a mile down the road on the right. Lovely place and the best food in the fens, with really nice rooms and no ghosts as far as I know.'

'Are you telling us that there are *two* Fishgutter's Arms?' asked Hettie, looking incredulous.

'Yes I am,' said Flavia, 'and if that's where you're supposed to be staying, you'll get a warm welcome from Scampi. You all look like you could do with a nice hot drink.'

It was a suggestion that all the cats could agree on. Flavia clambered back into the cab of her machine and returned with a bag that she passed to Betty. 'There you go – a couple of flasks in there to warm you all up. I made them up this morning in case I found anyone stranded.'

'You're a life saver!' said Beryl. 'We've got a good fire going in the bar here so why don't you join us and get warmed up a bit?'

Flavia was noticeably disturbed by the invitation and backed away towards her snow plough. 'That's kind of you, but wild horses and all the sheep in Lancashire wouldn't get me over that threshold. You should ask Scampi to explain why. I can't believe that you all spent the night there. I'd better get on – I've several miles of road to clear, but I might see you later at the proper Fishgutter's. If not, you can leave the flasks and the bag with Scampi – she'll pass them on. Happy Christmas again!'

Flavia leapt into her cab and was on her way before they had barely had time to wave. Betty led the way back to the bar, where the fire was burning low but still offering heat enough to thaw out their paws. The hot drinks were very welcome and the news of the real Fishgutter's Arms had lifted their spirits.

'Looks like we'll have a Christmas after all,' said Tilly joyfully as she offered her tin of Playbox Biscuits round to go with the milky tea. 'We'll be just in time for lunch at the other Fishgutter's if we get going soon.'

'Amen to that,' said Hettie, 'but we've got to get the Morris and Miss Scarlet started up first.'

Bruiser shook his head. 'I've got 'opes that Miss Scarlet will start, but I think we need ta give the distributor on the Morris a warm up ta get them spark plugs firin'. I'll go an' fetch it an' stick the empty 'amper on the back seat while I'm at it. We need ta be ready ta leave as soon as we get the engines goin'. At least we should 'ave a clear run now that Flavia's cleared the road.'

Bruiser left the warmth of the fire to see to the Butters' car. Tilly repacked her tartan shopper, putting the biscuits in the top, and Betty and Beryl buttoned their coats ready for departure. Lavender spent some time searching for something where she'd been sitting, tutting and talking to herself.

'Have you lost something?' asked Hettie, in a disinterested sort of way.

'It's my bag,' said Lavender. 'I must have left it upstairs.'

'Why don't you pop up and fetch it?' Hettie suggested, enjoying the look of fear that had suddenly appeared on the postmistress's face.

'If you think for one moment that I'm going into that room again you are very much mistaken. Mr Bruiser will have to go and fetch it when he returns.'

'I think Bruiser's a bit busy at the moment, trying to get us out of here, but I suppose I could go and look for you.'

It was a rare and triumphant moment to see Lavender Stamp display any form of gratitude towards Hettie – or any other cat for that matter – but she allowed herself to speak words she very seldom used. 'That is very good of you, thank you,' she said, almost under her breath.

'If you're going back up there I'm coming with you,' said Tilly, remembering the face she'd seen at the window and following Hettie towards the stairs. 'I don't think anyone should go up on their own.'

Hettie was glad of the company and the two friends climbed the stairs together, but what met them at the top was completely unexpected. The smell hit them first and reminded Tilly of one of those moments when the bonfire is lit on Guy Fawkes night. The vision before them was a blackened and charred mess. They moved forward, picking their way across the uneven floorboards. The doors to the rooms they'd so recently vacated were burnt to the floor and each of the small cells now opened out into one big, fire-damaged space, littered with ironmongery that had fallen away from the doors and blackened cast iron bedsteads that marked where the original rooms had been.

Hettie rubbed her eyes with her paws, trying to work out what had happened. 'This is unbelievable,' she said at last. 'How can there have been a fire up here without us noticing? Surely we'd have smelt the smoke, and what started it?'

Tilly had already backed away to the top of the stairs. 'Maybe one of our candles did it, but whatever has happened I think we should go now. You heard what Flavia said – this place is evil and I think the spirits are still here. I saw one of them up at the window when we were clearing the snow.'

'What do you mean you saw one of them?' asked Hettie, visibly alarmed.

'I saw a pale face at one of the windows, looking down on us,' said Tilly, 'but I didn't say anything because I didn't want to frighten everyone after what we all went through last night. I think it might have been Mrs Smith, but I'm not sure.'

'Then sod Lavender's bag! Let's go back downstairs and get the hell out of here as soon as we can. I don't understand what's happening in this place and I don't really want to.'

As Hettie made her way towards the top of the stairs, she noticed that there was something on one of the burnt-out beds and stopped briefly to investigate. There, in the blackened frame, nestled Lavender's overnight bag, completely untouched by the fire that had consumed everything else. Hettie snatched it from what was left of the old iron bed and returned to the corridor to join Tilly, but as she did so she was certain that she heard a voice behind her. 'She won't want to be without that, deary.'

Hettie didn't look back but continued to the top of the stairs, making a swift exit from the upper floor with Tilly leading the way. Lavender was almost grateful to be reunited with her bag and offered a very understated thank you. Bruiser had just finished warming the distributor cap from the Morris by the fire and announced that – with a bit of luck – they would soon be on their way. Hettie decided not to mention the state of the upper rooms as everyone gathered their things and assembled in the car park, keeping their paws crossed that the vehicles would cooperate. The Morris took some time to be coaxed into action but eventually it started and Betty revved the engine to keep it ticking over while they loaded their bags and Tilly's tartan shopper. Bruiser tried his luck with Miss Scarlet. The motorbike fired first time, getting a cheer from Hettie and Tilly as they clambered into the sidecar and closed the lid. With Lavender Stamp installed on the back seat of the Morris, Beryl hopped in beside her sister and they followed Miss Scarlet out of the car park towards what they hoped would be a proper Christmas dinner. As they left, six scowling faces stared down at them from the upper windows of The Fishgutter's Arms.

Chapter Eight
A Warm Welcome
with all the Trimmings

As Flavia Ashton had said, The Fishgutter's Arms was only a matter of a mile down the road. The surface that had recently been cleared was already beginning to freeze again as the sparkling winter sun receded, leaving a sky which threatened another bout of snow showers. On their way there, Hettie and Tilly had decided that they would say nothing to the others about their most recent experience on the upper floor of the old inn and that they would both enter into the true spirit of the season and enjoy themselves, leaving the ghosts of Christmas past behind them.

As Bruiser brought Miss Scarlet to a rather slippery halt in the car park, nothing could have been more different from their arrival the night before. Clearly Scampi Kelynack had pulled out all the festive stops to welcome her guests for the holiday. The surrounding trees were decorated with coloured lights and a magnificent sleigh, complete with reindeer and Santa Claws in all his red and white glory, stood out as a centrepiece in the pub's garden. The settled snow made the scene perfect and Tilly offered a squeal of delight as she pulled back the lid on the sidecar and hopped out, followed by Hettie.

Betty threw open the door on the Morris and purred with satisfaction as she slid towards the entrance of the pub, noting the welcoming light from within – every window festooned with bunches of holly and lanterns, offering a cheerful note to the season. Beryl was left to help Lavender out of the back of the car as Bruiser collected the luggage from the boot and the bag with Flavia's empty flasks from the sidecar.

Seeing that there were late arrivals, the ever-watchful Scampi Kelynack burst through the door to greet her newly arrived guests. 'You must be the Butters' party?' she said, with a pronounced Cornish accent. 'I've been proper worried, what with this snow an' everything.

Come in, my dears, an' get yourselves thawed out. Stick your coats here in the porch to dry. I've a lovely fire in the lounge an' my boy Jago,' she indicated a younger cat, 'will take your bags up to your rooms. Looks like you could all do with a cherry brandy to warm you up.'

At the mention of a cherry brandy Lavender thrust her valise at Jago and led the way into the lounge, where a number of guests sat around perusing the Christmas lunch menu. Scampi doled out the drinks and passed a pawful of menus to Betty to distribute amongst her party as they gratefully sank into the comfortable chairs. She relieved Bruiser of the bag with Flavia's flasks, promising to pass them on when she next saw her. 'Lunch will be at two so make yourselves at home. Your rooms are waiting for you if you'd like to freshen up. I'll be in the kitchen if anyone needs me. Sorry I can't stop an' chat but I'm up to my neck in stuffing.'

After Scampi had left, Hettie took in the scene in the lounge. The other guests were dressed in their Sunday best, as befitting Christmas Day, and she suddenly realised how bedraggled and scruffy they all were, having slept in their clothes and dug themselves out of a snowdrift. 'I think we should do as Scampi suggests and tidy ourselves up in our rooms,' she said, as discreetly as she could. 'We've got an hour before lunch.'

Having downed their cherry brandies, the six cats stood up and Jago – the cat who had disappeared with their luggage – presented himself at exactly the right moment to show them upstairs.

Betty had booked double rooms for herself and Beryl and for Hettie and Tilly, with two singles for Lavender and Bruiser. They couldn't have been more different from their most recent accommodation – warm and cosy and each with its own small decorated Christmas tree, a box of chocolates on the bed, tea and coffee making facilities and a festive tin of gingerbread cats on the tray with the mugs.

'Oooh, this is lovely!' said Tilly, trying out the bed she'd chosen. 'If it wasn't for Christmas lunch, I could curl up and sleep for a week.'

'I know what you mean,' said Hettie. 'Yesterday seems like a complete nightmare now, as if none of it really happened. I'm looking forward to a good night's sleep on a full stomach with all the trimmings that Scampi Kelynack can chuck at us, but we'd better tidy ourselves up first.'

Reluctantly, Tilly left the comfort of her bed and unpacked her tartan shopper, laying the clothes she'd brought out on Hettie's bed. The two cats pawed over them, selecting the most suitable combinations for a sit-down Christmas lunch. When they both looked a little more respectable, Tilly made two cups of milky tea and they sat on a couple of basket chairs by the window, looking out across the fen as the snow began to fall again. Hettie nibbled on a gingerbread cat while Tilly read from the menu card that Betty had given her. 'There's five courses!' she exclaimed in sheer delight. 'Whitebait for starters, followed by a prawn terrine, then comes the turkey, Brussels sprouts, roast potatoes and parsnips, carrots and roasted celery hearts. I suppose we have to have those as we're in the land of celery and carrots, but we've got bread sauce and stuffing as well. There's Christmas pudding next, with brandy butter and cream, followed by a cheese board. There's also a complimentary glass of fizzy, so that should please Lavender.'

'I doubt that only one glass will please her,' said Hettie. 'She downed that cherry brandy in one gulp and finished Beryl's off when she wasn't looking.'

'I suppose we'd better go down now that we look a bit nicer,' said Tilly. 'It's lovely here but it doesn't really feel like Christmas. I'm beginning to feel sorry for our tree and our presents back at home. I don't think I want to go away again and I keep thinking about those poor cats waiting to be hanged. I'm pleased we don't do that any more.'

'We did lots of things in our history that we shouldn't be proud of but, as you and I know, cats still like to murder other cats and I don't think that will ever change. Anyway, you'd better cheer up. Like it or not, it's Christmas and we need to make the most of it.'

Chapter Nine
Christmas Night

Christmas lunch was everything the menu cards promised. Scampi Kelynack excelled herself with every course, including a spectacular flaming Christmas pudding, so large that it had to be wheeled into the dining room on a trolley. There were silver sixpences for every guest, which made Tilly think back to the plight of Carlton Shortbread, but the lunch went without incident and the guests settled by the fire in the lounge afterwards to doze or play games of Cluedo and Scrabble.

Betty, Beryl and Lavender excused themselves from the after-lunch festivities to catch up on some sleep and enjoy the luxurious benefits of their four-star bedrooms. Hettie, Tilly and Bruiser claimed armchairs by the fire in the snug, a small but very comfortable room off the bar, and dozed until Scampi announced that a buffet of sandwiches and cake was laid out in the dining room for anyone who fancied a bite for Christmas tea or supper.

'I suppose we'd better show willing,' said Hettie, stretching and yawning. 'Even though I'm still full from lunch, it would be rude not to accept Scampi's invitation to her buffet.'

'I'll stay 'ere an' save the seats,' said Bruiser. 'You choose somethin' for me.'

Hettie and Tilly made their way into the dining room, where a long trestle table had been set up. No other guests had taken up the offer so they had the room to themselves. To say that Scampi's Christmas tea consisted just of sandwiches and cake was a bit of an understatement: the table groaned with every festive treat imaginable and Tilly wasted no time in quietly identifying each individual item, more for her own benefit than for Hettie's. 'We've got beef and turkey sandwiches,' she said, starting at the savoury end, 'a big ham, chicken drumsticks, small pies, although I'm not sure what's in them, cheese straws, sausage rolls, little sausages on sticks, something wrapped in bacon parcels, cheese puff balls and crisps. The sweets look lovely, too – look at that beautiful

Christmas cake with those little skaters on the top. I wonder if Scampi did that herself? And we've got mince pies, trifle and iced chocolate buns. Everything is just too lovely.'

Hettie was at a loss to know where to start, especially as she wasn't in the slightest bit hungry after such a big lunch, but she settled on a plate of beef sandwiches, getting the same for Bruiser. Tilly went for two chocolate buns and several little sausages on sticks and the two cats returned to the snug with their plates to find Bruiser fast asleep.

They returned to Scampi's buffet throughout the evening and dozed by the fire between courses, but there was no sign of the Butters or Lavender Stamp, who had found their rooms far too comfortable to leave. Warm, full and contented, Hettie was just considering the prospect of trying out the bed she had chosen when Scampi joined them in the snug and pulled up a chair by the fire. 'Flavia 'as just popped in to collect 'er flasks on 'er way back to 'er farm and she told me you'd 'ad to spend the night at the old Fishgutter's. I didn't realise you'd got that far. I thought you'd got stuck on the road this morning an' she'd rescued you. I just can't believe that you were in that awful place overnight, what with the so-called ghosts an' all. I keep meaning to 'ave the place pulled down.'

'I've got to admit it wasn't the best Christmas Eve,' said Hettie. 'We made the mistake of trying to sleep in the upstairs bedrooms.'

'What upstairs bedrooms?' said Scampi, looking alarmed. 'There aren't any bedrooms – not any more, anyway.'

'What do you mean?' asked Hettie, as Tilly and Bruiser sat up in their chairs, rubbing the sleep from their eyes and keen to hear what Scampi had to say.

'Those rooms were gutted in the fire back in eighteen something. No one 'as been in there since, except for the odd squatter, and they soon leave. I 'ad the place boarded up a while back while I decided what to do with it. Trouble is, I can't sell it – no one wants a supposedly haunted roadside inn with graves round the back.'

'I'm sorry,' said Hettie, 'but could you explain what happened there? We're all a bit confused.'

'Well, all I can tell you is that the old Fishgutter's used to be a holding place for thieves an' murderers back in Victorian times. The bedrooms you mentioned were nothing more than cells to keep the bad cats in. The story goes that one Christmas Eve there were five cats held there to be executed the next day at Gallows Edge by Ruben Catcraft, the hanging cat. It was one of those traditions to 'ave a mass hanging out on the fen – I think they did it at Easter, as well. Anyway, the cats they 'ad that Christmas Eve were all murderers an' locked up for the night. The landlord – a distant relative of mine – 'ad a full bar downstairs, as it was Christmas Eve. Just after midnight, a fire broke out upstairs. Some say it was Ruben Catcraft's pipe that started it. He was asleep an' got burnt to a cinder along with the five murderers locked in their rooms – poor things were roasted alive. The landlord managed to put out the fire an' stop it spreading downstairs, but it was too late for Ruben and his prisoners. They're all buried at the back of the old Fishgutter's, but according to the fen folk round 'ere those six cats haunt the place. Not that I've seen anything in there except spiders and cobwebs. I'm not one for believing in such silly tales.'

Hettie, Tilly and Bruiser sat silently for a few moments, taking in the story they'd just been told. Their encounters with the spirits now made perfect sense and no sense at all. So many questions ran through Hettie's mind. How was it that the bedrooms were there on Christmas Eve and destroyed by fire this morning? Did the ghostly re-enactment happen every Christmas Eve for unsuspecting travellers, or all year round? What purpose did the spirits have in appearing as they did and choosing to cling to the place where they had all died such a horrible death?

Scampi eventually broke the silence. 'So did you see any ghosts in there?' she asked. 'You mentioned the bedrooms?'

'Ah yes, well, we assumed there were bedrooms upstairs but you're absolutely right – it was all burnt out when we went up there and it did feel a bit spooky, so we lit a fire in the old bar and stayed there for the night.'

Tilly gave Hettie a quizzical look and Bruiser appeared even more bewildered; he had no idea what Hettie and Tilly had discovered when they had gone to fetch Lavender's bag.

Scampi stood up and yawned. 'I'd better get to my bed, as I've a busy day tomorrow looking after you all. I'm sorry you 'ad to spend the night in the old Fishgutter's and I'll make sure you get refunded, but at least the ghosts didn't bother you much – if there *are* any ghosts. The place having a reputation for being haunted is costing me money. I really must get it sorted in the New Year somehow – you're not the first guests to end up there by mistake, but I can't remember any of them actually spending the night before. I hope you all have a comfortable sleep. Breakfast is at ten in the dining room.'

'A bit spooky!' exclaimed Tilly after Scampi had left the snug. 'Why didn't you tell her what we all saw?'

'To be honest, I'm not sure what any of us saw or what was happening to us in that awful place and I didn't want us to look stupid,' said Hettie defensively. 'Scampi obviously doesn't believe in ghosts and I think we should keep what happened there to ourselves. At least we now know a bit more about the history of all those years ago, although why we were chosen to relive it we'll probably never know.'

'Some cats is highly tuned ta that sort of thing,' said Bruiser, 'an' we was there just at the right time of midnight on Christmas Eve, when accordin' ta Scampi the fire started. You, me an' Tilly 'ave all seen enough odd things in the past ta know that ghosts exist. Betty and Beryl are up for anythin' interestin' an' Lavender Stamp is weird anyway, so we're all perfect targets for the spirit world.'

'Irene Peggledrip says that it's only sensitive cats who have the gift of seeing spirits and that if we see one we should count ourselves really lucky,' said Tilly.

'I'm not sure where that leaves Lavender Stamp,' said Hettie, getting to her feet. 'There are lots of words I could use to describe her but "sensitive" isn't one of them.'

Bruiser and Tilly giggled and the three friends left the fire in the snug to enjoy a good night's sleep without visitations of any kind from the spirit world.

Chapter Ten
Six Tails in the Snow

Boxing Day passed in a party atmosphere of food, fun and congenial company. After several sherries, Lavender Stamp proved to be the life and soul of those gathered at the proper Fishgutter's Arms and it was with some reluctance that everyone packed up and headed homeward the next day. In spite of the cold temperatures, the Morris started first time and Miss Scarlet roared into life as soon as Bruiser asked. Flavia Ashton had made a good job of clearing the road and the fen looked magnificent as the morning sun kissed the deep drifts of snow, making them sparkle like crystals stretching out as far as the eye could see. The cathedral stood proud in the distance and owned every bit of its nickname as 'the ship of the fens', and the flatness of the land was suddenly beautiful in its winter blanket.

Scampi came out to wave her guests off on their journeys before returning to a mountain of washing up and changing beds ready for the New Year revellers to arrive. Hettie suggested that the Butters and Lavender steer a course for home; she wanted to stop off with Bruiser and Tilly at the old Fishgutter's, as she was interested in seeing the graves that Scampi had mentioned. The Butters offered no resistance and Betty noticeably put her foot down as the Morris passed the inn, leaving Miss Scarlet to slide into the car park.

The old pub looked as bleak as ever. Bruiser was keen to see the burnt-out bedrooms upstairs that Hettie had described to Scampi and he left Hettie and Tilly to make their way round to the back. At first there was nothing to see but more deep drifts and a substantial holly bush, its boughs hung low with the weight of the snow. The bush boasted a stunning array of red berries that stood out magnificently against the white backdrop of the surrounding fen. A robin danced from one branch to another, singing its heart out.

'I can't see anything that looks like graves,' said Hettie, stamping her feet to keep warm and causing the startled robin to take flight. 'Maybe they don't have stones and are just buried here under the snow, as most of them were murderers. Perhaps whoever buried them at the time decided that they didn't deserve to have marked graves.'

Tilly shuffled forward to take a closer look and shrank back immediately, nearly knocking Hettie off her feet. 'Look!' she said. 'There's tracks in the snow from over there, all leading back to the inn.'

Hettie went forward to investigate and counted six sets of footprints. She followed one of them, which ended abruptly in the middle of nowhere. In spite of the cold, she scrabbled in the snow and uncovered what was clearly a grave stone. Tilly followed her and the two cats set about clearing the snow from where the footprints stopped. Having seen the burnt-out upper storey for himself, Bruiser came out to help and before long they had uncovered six graves. The names were faded but just about discernible and the date on all the stones was very clear: 25th December 1877. Tilly read out the names as a roll call. 'Theodora Smith, Millicent Rumble, Agnes Buckle, Jabari Cook, Ruben Catcraft and Jack Hawks.'

A great sadness suddenly descended upon the three cats and Hettie slid over to the holly bush to pull six small sprigs from it, laden with berries. She placed one at the base of each of the stones, remembering that the Druids regarded holly as sacred and a protection against evil spirits. The friends bowed their heads in a mark of respect, then turned to make their way back to Miss Scarlet.

'And now for an "at-home Christmas",' said Tilly, settling herself in the sidecar next to Hettie and closing the lid. Bruiser kicked the motorbike into life just as the snow began to fall again. As they left the car park, six faces watched them from the windows of the pub and this time they were smiling.

Acknowledgements

As an arts journalist I had the pleasure of producing a series of programmes on the myths and legends of the Cambridgeshire Fens. Some of those stories have stayed with me and have inspired me to create the characters within this book. The fens are a good case for 'Marmite': some find them magical and strangely beautiful; others forbidding and depressing; the one attribute they do possess in shedloads is atmosphere – a wonderful tool for any writer.

The Fishgutter's Arms is straight out of my own experience of booking accommodation and finding the pub derelict and boarded up on arrival. I never did get my money back.

Thank you to Pete Duncan and all at Farrago Books, and to my irreplaceable editor Abbie Headon; it's always a joy to share these journeys with her. Thank you to Catriona Robb for her keen eye and to Jason Anscomb for another fine cover. Finally to Barbara Erskine, the Queen of Ghosts, for taking time to read and comment on this book in the spirit it was written, and to Nicola for her love and support as deadlines approach.

About the Author

Mandy Morton was born in Suffolk. After a short and successful music career in the 1970s as a singer-songwriter – during which time she recorded six albums and toured extensively throughout the UK and Scandinavia with her band – she joined the BBC, where she produced and presented arts-based programmes for local and national radio. She more recently presents The Eclectic Light Show on Mixcloud.com.

Mandy lives with her partner, who is also a crime writer, in Cambridge and Cornwall, where there is always room for a long-haired tabby cat. She is the author of The No. 2 Feline Detective Agency series and also co-wrote *In Good Company* with Nicola Upson, which chronicles a year in the life of Cambridge Arts Theatre. A complete retrospective collection of Mandy's music entitled *After The Storm* has recently been released on Cherry Red Records.

Twitter: **@hettiebagshot** and **@icloudmandy**
Facebook: **HettieBagshotMysteries**

Preview

The Tabby in Black

Chocks away! as our feline detectives investigate some sticky situations at the local chocolate factory in Catberry-on-the-Brink.

Up at the Manor House, the family is at war as dark secrets are uncovered in The Tabby in Black chocolate selection box.

Will Hettie and Tilly manage to reach the bottom layer before a murderer strikes? Did Horace Catberry really choke on a Mog Nob biscuit? And will the Goth Band Gums and Noses get to support The Travelling Whoopsies on their next tour?

Join Hettie and Tilly as they unwrap the mysteries swirling around the Catberry family in this bitter-sweet assortment of truth and lies.

COMING SOON

Also available

The No. 2 Feline Detective Agency begins

Hettie Bagshot has bitten off more than any cat could chew. No sooner has she launched her detective agency than she's thrown into her first case.

Furcross, home for senior cats, has a nasty spate of bodysnatching, and three former residents have been stolen from their graves. Hettie and her sidekick, Tilly, set out to reveal the terrible truth. Is Nurse Mogadon involved in a deadly game?

In a haze of catnip and pastry, Hettie steers the case to its conclusion, but will she get there before the body count rises – and the pies sell out?

OUT NOW

Also available

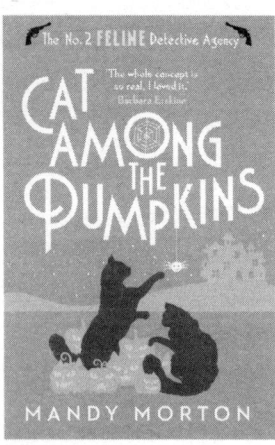

Gunpowder, treacle and shocks

As All Hallows' Eve approaches, Hettie Bagshot of The No. 2 Feline Detective Agency has more than just a ghost and a warlock tart on her plate.

Upon discovering the body of Mavis Spitforce, Hettie and her trusty sidekick, Tilly, set out to investigate an old crime and a spate of new murders. Why was Mavis Spitforce dressed for Halloween? And what's the connection to the legend of Milky Myers, suspected of murdering his family on Halloween, longer ago than anyone can remember?

As the November fog closes in, can the tabby duo unearth the truth, and stop the murderer before they strike again – and will there be enough samosas to go round?

OUT NOW

Also available

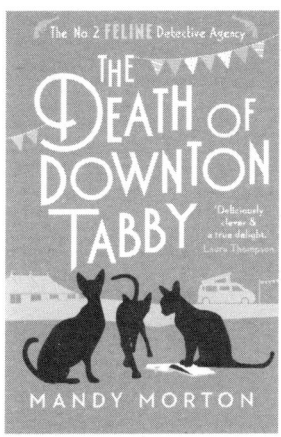

Hettie and Tilly are on the case

The town is celebrating its first literary festival, and The No. 2 Feline Detective Agency has been hired to oversee security.

When the body of the most popular author, Sir Downton Tabby, is found in a secluded part of the grounds, Hettie and her faithful sidekick Tilly are plunged into crisis as a serial killer stalks the festival.

As the duo turn their attention to investigating the death of Downton Tabby, will there be an author left standing? Will Meridian Hambone sell out of her 'Littertray' t-shirts? And will there be enough crime teas to go around?

OUT NOW

Also available

A murder mystery party goes off the rails

Hettie and Tilly are invited to host a Christmas Eve murder mystery aboard the Santa Claws Express. No sooner has the train left the station at Mogbury-on-the-Tilt than our two feline detectives are caught up in a murderous family feud between the Shuttles and the Stokers.

Is the ghost of Hornby Stoker haunting the line? And will Hettie and Tilly's Christmas be derailed?

Join our tabby heroes as they plough their way through red herrings, hot chestnuts and snowbound platforms in a hunt for a festive fiend who will stop at nothing.

OUT NOW

Note from the Publisher

To receive updates on new releases in The No. 2 Feline Detective Agency series – plus special offers and news of other humorous fiction series to make you smile – sign up now to the Farrago mailing list at farragobooks.com/sign-up.